Celebrity

KATHLEEN SQUIRE-MEROLLA

Outskirts Press, Inc.
Denver, Colorado

Outskirts Press, Inc.
http://www.outskirtspress.com

ISBN: 978-1-4327-5627-7

Outskirts Press and the "OP" logo are trademarks belonging to Outskirts Press, Inc.

PRINTED IN THE UNITED STATES OF AMERICA

For my family and friends,
Thank you for your your
help and encouragement.
I love you all!

Chapter One
The Disgrace
Summer 1997

he sun was slowly making its way higher in the azure, early July sky. The temperature was rising quickly to an uncomfortable 90 degrees for the third day in a row; a heat wave, according to the meteorologist on the radio station Lora was singing along with. Lora Logan had been out of school for two weeks and was growing bored with summer. Most of her friends were either away on vacation or attending some sort of summer camp. Lora was planning to attend music camp the second week of August She loved music, and at fourteen, was an accomplished pianist. She had been playing since she was five years old.

Lora was washing the breakfast dishes as it was one of the daily chores her mother expected her to complete before she did anything else. Lora's mother, Janice, was a real estate broker and her father, David, was a stone mason working with the Engels Construction Company. They lived in a modest side hall colonial on a cul-de-sac in Latham, New York. It is the only home Lora has ever known. She just completed the eighth grade and was looking forward to entering high school in the fall. Lora was placing the last of the silverware in the drawer when her cell phone rang. Lora had been grounded, and she knew it was her mother calling to check on her. She hoped her mother was in a good mood. Lora hoped to be un-grounded this afternoon; therefore, she was rushing to get all of her chores done.

"Hi, Mom." Lora pushed the drawer shut with her hip as she held the phone to her ear with her right hand. She placed the blue, plaid towel through the handle on the stove to dry. She headed to her bedroom as she listened to her mother.

"Yes, I did the dishes and emptied the trash." She sighed as she answered her mother's question. "I cleaned up my room and made my bed." Lora rolled her eyes. Luckily her mother wasn't there to see her. She hated when Lora did that. She said it was disrespectful. "Am I off restriction now?" she asked, hopefully. She didn't wait for her mother to answer. "Mommy, could I call Emma and see if she can go swimming with me?" Lora asked in her sweetest voice. It was the voice she always used when she wanted something. "I'll be home by 4:00. I promise."

Lora waited for her mother to answer. She prayed the answer would be "yes". She had been grounded since the weekend for not taking her mother's call, when she was at the mall with Emma. She knew she was running late and pretended her cell phone battery was too low to answer the phone. Actually, she was visiting with friends in the food court and didn't want to leave. As she was explaining this to her mother, when she got home later that day, her cell phone started ringing. Her mother took it from her and saw a full set of power bars. She had kept the phone and told Lora she could have it back the following Saturday, which was today. Janice had left Lora's phone out on the kitchen counter before she left for work.

Her mother hadn't answered yet, so she pleaded, "Please Mommy. It's *sooo* hot today."

All the local kids knew about the swimming hole on Murray's farm. It had been used for irrigation when the farm was operational. Now, Mr. Murray let the kids swim there if they didn't leave debris or play loud music. The kids were respectful to Mr. Murray, because they were so thankful to be allowed to swim there. A couple of the boys had climbed the large oak tree, on the bank of the pond, and tied a rope to a branch that reached out over the pond, about eight feet above the water. They tied an old tire at the bottom of the rope to serve as a swing which allowed them to drop into ten feet of water.

"Sorry, Honey. I have a client at my desk. Yes, you and Emma may go swimming, if all of your chores are finished. You promise to be home by four?" Janice finally answered her daughter who was excitedly pulling her new aqua, two-piece bathing suit from a Macy's shopping bag. Lora had purchased it last Saturday. She held her phone pinned to her shoulder with her cheek.

"I promise, Mommy! Thank you. I have to call Emma. Bye Bye." Lora always called her mother "Mommy" when she was being endearing and was pleased with her latest conquest of getting off restriction.

Janice barely got "Bye" out when the phone went dead. She smiled at herself as she laid the cell phone on her desk. Her only child was so responsible for her age. She got all A's and Janice hoped she wasn't too hard on her. Like all mothers Janice only wanted the best for her daughter and felt guilty that Lora had to spend so much time alone. Lora had won the lead in the school musical this past year, and Janice asked her if she would like to attend music would help to break up the summer. Janice made the arrangements.

Lora would be going to Skye Farm in August. Janice knew Lora was excited about it. Her clients broke her train of thought with a question, on the form they were filling out. Janice would be calling Lora, to check in with her, if she didn't hear from her first, within the next two hours.

Lora wasted no time calling Emma Masters. Of course Emma was thrilled to have her best friend off restriction and would "love to go swimming." They made plans to meet at Emma's house and ride their bikes the three miles to the pond. Lora hurried to get into her new bathing suit, She looked at herself in the full length mirror that was fastened to the inside of her bedroom door. She smiled with satisfaction. Lora had shoulder length, dark brown wavy hair and green eyes. Her dark complexion had only the beginning of a summer tan. She had the body of a young woman and looked older than her years. "You go girl!" she said to herself. After applying suntan lotion, she threw on a yellow knit, sleeveless sun-dress over the suit, before slipping on a matching pair of novelty, toe loop, flip-flops. She grabbed the small black, nylon back-pack hanging on the desk chair by her window, and stuffed a towel and her cell phone inside. Lora zipped it shut and shoved her arms through the straps. She picked her sunglasses off the desk and left the room. Lora snatched the back door key from its kitchen hook and took a water bottle from the fridge. She slipped an arm from the back pack, put the water bottle inside with the towel, re-zipped it, and shoved her arm back threw the strap. Lora walked to the front door, made sure it was locked, and then, went to the garage off of the kitchen to get her bike and helmet. She pressed the code to open the over-head door and walked her bike out with her helmet hanging on the handle bar. After closing the overhead door, Lora secured the chin strap on her helmet. She swung her leg over the seat and peddled down the driveway, turning left at the end toward Emma 's house. Emma lived three streets over and was waiting at the end of her driveway when Lora rode up minutes later.

"Hi Emma. It sure is hot."

"I'm so glad you aren't being punished any more. I was so bored. Jillian is away with her family and Brittney, Meghan and Patty are at Girl Scout camp for two weeks." The girls headed down the road and waved to Emma's mother who was standing in the doorway.

"Yeah, I got a post card from Patty yesterday. I guess they're having a great time." Lora told Emma.

The girls shared all their latest gossip as they peddled their way to the farm. They took their time because of the heat, which was even hotter out on the open blacktop. Emma's mother had French braided her sandy colored hair and Lora pulled her shoulder length, dark brown, wavy hair back into a ponytail. Their foreheads were beaded with perspiration and ran into Emma's blue eyes as they happily rode along side-by-side. They began singing Elton John's "Candle in the-Wind" and were just finishing the last verse when they reached the dirt path that ran through the back of the farm.

This all use to be a corn field but now only weeds remained on either side of the narrow dirt road. The path was just wide enough for the girls to ride side-by-side, each in a worn tire track. Little patches of grass and weeds grew between the tracks. The weeds were three feet high on each side of Lora and Emma. They hopped off of their bikes long enough to pick a few wild black raspberries that were growing along the side of the path. Their lips were stained red from the berries which made them laugh at each other. They got back on their bikes, and as they rounded the bend, the pond came into view.-The murky water glistened in the sun and looked cool and inviting. The only shade was from an old oak tree.

The tall weeds surrounded a pond that was about forty feet across and a hundred feet long. The weeds had been trampled by previous pond users. The girls peddling a little quicker, hopped off their bikes leaving them in the weeds where they had dismounted.

Lora took off her backpack and pulled out her water bottle and towel. She threw the towel over her shoulder, unscrewed the top of the, now, lukewarm water, took a long drink. She then offered some to Emma. "At least it's wet." she said after taking a drink.

"Thanks, Lora, I'm dying of the heat. Can't wait to hit the water." Emma drank some water and handed the bottle back to Lora. Lora screwed the top on and dropped it onto the backpack that lay on her bike.

"Last one in the water is a rotten egg." she yelled as she discarded her dress, flip-flops, and towel into a pile on the bikes.

No one else was around yet. The girls ran the last few feet in the soft dirt and leaped into the water, feet first. They both sunk below the surface with a big splash leaving two large wakes that eventually made their way to the shore line. A few moments later both girl's heads popped to the surface, as they laughed and bobbed in the water. The water was eighty degrees, yet felt refreshing on their hotter bodies.

"This is heaven," Lora said, floating on her back with her eyes closed, arms outstretched, and her pony tail fanning out around her head.

Emma was swimming to shore and called back to the floating body. "Yeah, this is great!" Emma scampered up the bank and headed to the tire swing, dripping water from her body that turned the dirt beneath her to mud. She put her right, muddy foot into the tire, and hopped back as far as the rope would allow, in order to get a good swing out over the water. "Look out below!" she yelled, as she sailed out over the pond, giggling the whole time. Lora, anticipating where Emma would land, began swimming to the ponds edge, deciding she too would like to try the swing. She got to the base of the tree in time to see Emma squeal and splash into the water, sinking deep below the surface. Lora reached out to grab the tire as it swung back to shore. She threw one leg over the top of the tire preferring to sit in top of it for her ride out to the water.

Like Emma, Lora hopped back to allow for a perfect swing. She threw her other leg over the tire and sailed forward over the water. Feeling the cool breeze on her wet skin, Lora decided not to flop off of the tire on the first swing, preferring to swing back and forth two more times. Then she let go of the rope. She fell backwards into the water, causing a huge splash as she hit the water with her full back. She had leaned a little too far back. When she resurfaced, she had a pained look on her face.

"Are you all right?" Emma asked, as she stood on the bank, holding the tire in her two hands.

"Wow! That hurt!" Lora said, as she slowly swam to the ponds edge. When she got next to Emma she turned her back towards her friend. "Is it very red?"

Emma winced, "It's the shade of a cooked lobster, girl. Ow, painful."

"I think I'll go feet first next time. Want to go together Emma?"

"Yeah, sure climb on."

They both put one foot in the tire and hopped backwards to launch themselves over the water. They screamed as they sailed over the water and let go simultaneously, with Lora hitting the water slightly ahead of Emma. The girls resurfaced and instantly began laughing. They decided to play a little Marco Polo.

"Not it." Lora shouted slightly ahead of Emma.

"OK." Emma turned her back and began counting to twenty before shouting, "Marco." with her eyes closed.

Somewhere in the distance Lora replied, "Polo." Emma swam in the direction of the reply with her eyes closed. She repeated the process of shouting " Marco" and reached in the direction of the reply "Polo" from Lora. They took turns being *it,* and after about an hour in the water, decided to lay on their towels to rest. They wearily climbed out of the water and spread their towels, side by side, on the scrub grass and dirt, on the pond's bank. Lora sighed as she lay her dripping body face down on her oversize, striped beach towel. "I'm exhausted."

"I could use a little nap myself," Emma said, sitting down on the towel she had spread next to Lora's. She lay back with her knees bent up to the sky. "This was a great idea. Thanks for calling me. And thank you, Mrs. Logan for letting Lora off restriction!"

"I couldn't stand staying in the house another day. I promised that I would be home by 4 PM. I can't be late." Lora's green eyes where closed as she spoke. "I should probably call and let my mother know we're fine. I want to keep her happy. You know how that goes."

"Do you want me to get your pack?"

"Gee, thanks Emma."

"Could I call my mom when you're through? I have to keep her happy too." Emma gave a little laugh as she got up to go get the pack from the bikes a few feet from where they were. Emma picked up the back-pack, took it over to Lora and set it next to her. "Here you go."

"I'll just be a minute." Lora pressed the numbers on her phone pad and waited for her mother to answer. "Hi Mom. Emma and I are just taking a little break from the water, so I thought I'd give you a call." Lora was rummaging through her pack in search of the wide tooth comb she knew she kept there. "OK mom, I won't be late." She found the comb. "Yes, pizza sounds good. I'll be starving." She set the comb on her towel and pulled the ponytail holder from her wet hair. "I love you too. Bye." Lora ended her call, handed the phone to Emma, put the pony tie on her wrist, and began to comb out her long wet hair.

"Hi mom. Lora let me borrow her phone so I could let you know we're fine." Emma smiled at Lora and gave a wink as she raised her shoulders to her ears in a quick movement. "We'll be home by 4 PM." There was a pause as she listened to her mother. " Mom, I'm always careful." Emma rolled her eyes. "Yes, I love you too, mom. I have to go. Bye Bye." Emma closed the phone and handed it back to Lora. "Thanks. I hope that earned me some points." She lay on her back and closed her eyes to the sun.

Lora set the phone on her towel and lay on her stomach placing her folded arms under her cheek. She began to hum, "How Do I Live." After a few bars Emma joined in, still laying with her eyes shut. They lay there humming the song, until they heard a snap. Opening their eyes, they both heard the sound and stopped humming. Emma sat up and looked around.

Lora lifted her head and looked at Emma. "What was that?"

"Don't know." She continued to look around. "Anybody there? Maybe someone else is coming for a swim?"

There was no reply. Then, from the tall weeds emerged a tall, good-looking guy. He had short blond hair and was wearing large sunglasses, making him appear very "Hollywood." He held a green beer bottle, in one hand, and a red and white cooler in the other. He stumbled as he walked towards them. "Hello ladies. Hot as hell today. You two look pretty comfortable." He took a long swig from the beer bottle. "You ladies want a cold beer?" He was standing over them. They couldn't see his eyes through his dark glasses, but they knew they had never seen him before.

"We don't drink." Lora told the stranger.

"Suit yourselves. More for me." He sat down in the dirt at the girl's feet. He was wearing cut-off jeans and brown sandals. There was a white, sleeveless, tee-shirt hanging from his back pocket. He had a black shoulder bag over one shoulder. He had a lean, muscular build. "Haven't seen you lovely ladies around school."

"You aren't looking in the right school." Emma giggled. Emma always giggled when she was nervous, and good looking guys made her nervous.

"Oh? What school do you go to?"

"Colonie Middle School, but we are going to high school in the fall. Where do you go?" Lora asked.

"I just graduated college." He took another drink from the bottle, while he looked the girls up and down. "You look older. Sure you aren't in college?"

Emma giggled again. "We're going into the ninth grade in September. What's your name?"

He smiled at her showing his perfect white teeth that looked even whiter against his dark tanned face. Perspiration glistened on his broad muscular chest. He took some time before answering, "My friends call me Smilin' Jack. What's yours?" Doug Civics did not use his real name. He was pouring on the charm, and could tell it was working; it always did.

"I'm Emma and this is my best friend, Lora." Emma looked at Lora when she said her name.

"Nice to meet you. What do you two do for fun, besides

swimming that is?" He drained the beer bottle, set it into the cooler, and picked out another. He closed the cooler, twisted the top off, and took another drink. He never took his eyes off of the girls.

Lora was beginning to feel a little uncomfortable. She sat up now and pulled her knees up to her chest.

Emma was sitting crossed legged and leaned slightly forward, toward Doug, as if she was very interested in what he had to say. "We like music." She told him.

"That's cool. Who do you like?"

"We like LeAnn Rimes, Back Street Boys, and Puff Daddy."

"Didn't I hear you humming, 'How Do I Live', just now?"

Emma giggled again. "Yes." She looked to Lora for her reaction. Lora wasn't smiling. She realized Lora hadn't said more than a few words since the stranger arrived. She gave her a puzzled look.

Doug finished off the bottle of beer he had just opened and put the empty bottle into the cooler with the others. "I couldn't drink during training."

"Training?" Emma asked.

"Yeah, I was on the football team." Doug smiled at them, again, knowing that he was impressing them. "My hobby is photography. Doug slid the shoulder bag off of his shoulder and pulled out a digital camera. Mind if I take your picture?" Doug took off his glasses, revealing the lightest, ice blue eyes Lora had ever seen. He held up the camera and looked through it. "Beautiful!"

Emma began to giggle again. "I think I'd rather go for a swim." Lora said. She hopped up quickly, jumped off the edge of the pond, and disappeared into the water. Emma hopped up and followed her friend.

Doug smiled and set the camera back into the bag. *Time for that later.* He slipped off his sandals and removed his cut-offs. He jumped into the water, naked, before the girls came to the surface. When he surfaced, he shook his head like a dog, sending water droplets flying all around his head. "Ah, this is refreshing."

In the murky water the girls hadn't noticed that he was nude, yet. He swam towards Emma, grabbed her, and tossed her backwards into the water. She came up sputtering, then began laughing. "Hey, you stop that," she said, kidding around.

"What's the matter. Don't you want to play?" Doug was swimming towards her again. He caught Emma and told her to put her foot in his waist high, clasped hands, so that he could launch her into the air. Emma, being young and naïve, played along. She held onto Doug's solid shoulders, put her foot into his hands, and let him hoist her into the air. She sailed up and backwards, landing into the water. "Do it again," she squealed, swimming back towards him.

"Yeah sure. Let's let Lora have a turn." Doug said. He started to swim towards Lora who was treading water a few feet away.

"That's all right Let Emma go again."

"Are you sure?" Doug was treading water next to Lora now. His leg brushed hers.

Emma was in front of Doug now. She put her hands on his broad shoulders and bent her knee to put her foot into Doug's hands. Her foot brushed against his aroused manhood, but she was totally unaware. Doug launched her into the air, once again, as she squealed with delight. Lora watched her friend and smiled at Emma's joy. Doug was watching Lora, with those blue eyes, and smiling. "Sure you don't want to try it?" He asked her again. *What a cold fish she is.* He thought.

"No thanks. I really have to be going home now. My mother's expecting me."

"What's the hurry? Aren't you having fun?" Doug grabbed her around her waist and spun her around in a circle. His hands *accidentally* brushed Lora's perky breasts. "Are you sure you aren't in high school?" Doug put his mouth close to Lora's ear. "You sure look hot." He continued to hold her close to his body by her breasts. He didn't like rejection.

Emma swam back eager to fly again. "See, your friend wants to play." He said into Lora's ear, so only she could hear.

"Let me go!" Lora struggled to get free.

"What's going on?" Emma asked almost out of breath from all her swimming back and forth.

"Lora doesn't want to play. She wants to go home." Still Doug was holding her, only tighter, causing Lora discomfort when she tried to move. She was trying to pry his strong arm off her body.

"Please, let me go!"

"What's wrong with you Lora? I want to do it again." She tried to hang onto Doug's shoulders but Lora was in the way. "Please toss me again."

"Yeah, sure." Doug, reluctantly, let Lora go, and prepared to toss Emma again, if only to get rid of her. As soon as he let Lora go, she headed to the bank. Doug quickly tossed Emma as far as he could and was right behind Lora in seconds. He grabbed her around the waist and pulled her close again. His aroused manhood was pushing between her legs. Lora began kicking to get free. "Let me go!" she screamed at him. The kicking and squirming only aroused Doug more. He really got off on having power and control.

"Now you want to play. OK, I want to play too." He whispered to her. Doug pulled Lora up the bank and over to her towel, while she kicked and punched at his strong arms around her waist, but to no avail. She scraped her legs on some tree limbs on the shore.

Emma reached the bank just as Doug threw Lora to the towel and sat on top of her, holding her arms to the ground over her head. "Hey, you let her go. This isn't funny." She came up behind Doug and tried to pull him from Lora.

Doug back handed Emma across the face. She fell backwards, and hitting her head on a rock, she lay unconscious in the dirt. "Wait your turn girl" He sneered, not giving her a second look. "Smilin' Jack has plenty to go around."

Doug had Lora pinned to the towel, as she continued to squirm to get free. He kissed her roughly. Lora was crying and trying to shake her head from side to side to avoid his mouth. "Now let's see those beautiful breasts of yours. He gave the string at the neck of her top a sharp yank, and it broke. "MMMM. Very nice Miss Lora." He rubbed his face on her soft flesh and sighed. His rough stubble scratched her skin. He gave her breast a small bite on her hard nipple. Lora started to scream out in pain, but Doug smothered her face with his large hand. "Now, Now. You'd better be quiet. What else do you have hidden?" He once again yanked at Lora's bathing suit bottom, and it tore at the side seam. "Well, Well. Look what I found." He kissed her mouth hard again to keep her quiet. She cut the inside of her lip on her teeth. "Won't do you any good to struggle." He slapped her across the face. "Stay still and shut up bitch. I am trying to teach you something, here."

Lora was terrified. Her face stung where he had slapped her. She could taste blood inside her mouth. She saw her cell phone laying just out of reach. Doug had ahold of both her hands in his left hand and was holding them above her head. His right hand was groping her young body; pinching, squeezing and twisting. Exploring every inch of her young, delicate skin. Lora tried to scream in pain, but she always found her mouth covered with his foul tasting mouth.

When he hit her, she saw stars for a moment, and went quiet with fear. All she could think about was getting her phone and calling *'Mommy, please help me'*, she thought. She could smell the alcohol with every foul word, every breath, and every kiss. It made her sick to her stomach. She was afraid she would throw up and he would be even madder. She knew she was going to die, here.

Doug had removed Lora's bathing suit completely, tossing it aside in the mud. She lie there, vulnerable to his desire. She tried to squirm out of his grip, but he hit her again, this time causing her eye to begin to swell shut. He was roughly pushing her legs apart with his knee. "Come on bitch. You're going to like this. I bet you're a virgin. I know I'm going to love it." He lowered all of his weight down on Lora and pulled her leg over, with one strong hand, to make room for his pleasure. He began thrusting and pushing until he got all of himself inside and began to moan and sigh. "Oh yeah. See bitch, I told you you would love it." It was over in seconds but to Lora it felt like an eternity.

Lora felt crushed beneath Doug's body. She could barely breathe. She felt his vice like grip on her leg, twisting and pulling at her. Then the sharp pain as he pushed over and over until she thought he had ripped her apart. She tried to scream, but he covered her mouth with his once again. He was sucking the youth right out of her. Lora thought she was dying. She had stopped fighting and lay still, picturing her mother and father and praying for them to come and save her. She couldn't see out of her eye and squeezed the good eye shut, trying to shut what was happening out of her mind.

Doug satisfied himself in seconds and lay, unmoving, on top of Lora. He was breathing heavily, and his heart was beating fast. "Yeah, baby. Give me a minute and we can play again. Looks like your friend gave up. It's just you and me, kid."

Lora didn't hear a word he was saying. She had gone to a quiet place inside herself. She was singing along with the music in her mind.

"Ah, you're no fun." The fight was gone from Lora and so, too, was Doug's pleasure.

Lora was still in her musical world and only saw and felt the music.

Doug had lost interest with Lora and dove back into the water. When he came back out he dressed, and as an afterthought took some pictures of the naked Lora and the unconscious Emma. Lora had ceased to feel. She couldn't see clearly. But that voice and those eyes were burned into her mind forever. Doug got bored and finally left back through the tall weeds; the same way he had arrived, carrying his camera bag and cooler. He was whistling. Emma still lay unconscious, next to Lora, where he left her. Lora lay naked, battered, and bleeding on the rumpled towel in he mud. Dirt caked to her drying hair and bloodied face. Her soft delicate skin was swollen and bruised.

Suddenly the cell phone began to ring. It was Janice. Lora was in shock but she reached for her phone out of instinct. She opened the phone; her mother was shouting, "Lora where are you? You promised you would be home a half hour ago. Lora, answer me!" Lora couldn't answer but began to cry at the sound of her mother's voice. "Lora? Is that you Lora? Oh my God Baby! I'm coming." The line went dead.

Lora tried to say "Mommy" but she didn't have the strength.

After hanging up her phone, Janice called her husband and told him of the disturbing call. "I think she's still at that swimming pond, David. I'm going there now."

"I'll meet you there." David rushed to his truck and raced to the

Murray farm. Speed limits be damned.

Janice was all ready in her car and speeding down the road. She got to the dirt road first and drove as fast as she could. She stopped short when she saw the bikes laying on their sides, and a heap of clothes confirming her suspicion that they were there. A dirt cloud swirled around in the air from her sudden stop, obliterating her view of the scene, temporarily. Janice left the car running, drivers door open, and sprinted the short distance to the pond. She screamed when she saw the naked little girl lying in the dirt on the ground. She hurried to her daughter's side and felt for a pulse. "My poor baby!" Janice, satisfied that her daughter was alive, turned her attention to Emma.

David's truck came plowing down the road, spewing dirt and weeds into the air. He slammed on his brakes, and flew from the truck, calling Janice's name. He stopped short at the horrifying scene before him. "NOOOOO!" he yelled.

Janice looked up, her face wet with tears. "They're alive! Call 911."

Stunned, David reached for his cell phone, dialing 911, while he continued to hurry to his family's sides. "Yes, I'm at the Murray farm." He paused, "down the back field. Two girls, one unconscious." He paused again. "Please hurry! Yes, I'll stay on the line." David knelt next to his wife and child. He smoothed the hair back from the battered face of his daughter. "Put this on her." David began to remove his shirt. Janice helped him and put the blue, cotton, button shirt on Lora, who moaned, "Mommy?"

"Yes baby, Mommy and Daddy are here. You're safe now." Janice held her in her arms and rocked her. Tears were running down her cheeks. She looked at David. "Who could have done this?"

David was still holding the cell phone. "Yes I hear the ambulance in the distance." He said to the person on the other end of the phone." He hung up and turned his attention to Emma. He kept a small blanket over the back seat of his truck and ran to get it. He wrapped Emma in it and noticed the blood on the back of her head. The ambulance had arrived and paramedics were approaching, quickly. One asked what had happened.

"It appears to be a sexual assault." David choked on the words "She has a head wound." He indicated holding the blanket wrapped Emma." David lay her down so that the paramedic could tend to her. The second paramedic was tending to Lora. When the girls were stabilized, they put Emma on a stretcher and loaded her into the waiting ambulance. Dave insisted on following behind with Lora, himself.

Janice was calling Emma's mother to tell her what had happened. She told her to meet them at Memorial hospital. Within forty-five minutes the two sets of parents were in the waiting-room, awaiting news of their daughters' conditions. "Who could have done this ?" was repeated over and over by the assembled, bewildered parents.

The police had arrived having been alerted to the incident, when the 911 call had come in. They were waiting to speak to the girls.

A doctor came out. "Mr. and Mrs. Logan?"

David and Janice turned, David with his arm around his wife. "Yes." he said. "How is she?"

The doctor moved closer to the couple to speak more privately. "Please come with me." He led them to Lora's door. "Your daughter will recover physically. She's in shock right now, and we would like to keep her overnight for observation."

"May I go in?" Janice asked. The tears were glistening in her eyes.

"Certainly. She needs your support." He handed Janice a card.

"This is the name of a rape counselor. It would be good to have Lora speak to a professional, as soon as possible."

"Thank you, Doctor." David took the card and put it in his pants pocket. Janice was already opening the door to go to Lora's bed. David followed. "She looks so small and helpless."

"She is." Janice said. "I should have been there for her. "I shouldn't have left her alone so much."

"Don't start blaming yourself. Even if you were home you would have let her go swimming. I'm as much as fault as you are."

Janice was holding Lora's hand, when Lora flickered her eye; then opened it to see her mother and father standing over her.

"Mommy? Daddy?"

"Yes, we're still here." Janice kissed Lora lightly on her forehead.

"Hey, sweetie." David kissed her, also, and smoothed her bruised cheek with his hand. "Can you tell us what happened, honey?" Tears began to run from Lora's eyes, down the side of her swollen face, and onto the white pillow under her head. She squeezed them tightly. David wiped the wetness away with his thumb. "It's OK if you can't tell us. The police want to talk to you, though. Will you talk to them?"

Suddenly, Lora popped her good eye open, "Where's Emma?" she breathed softly.

"Emma's here. She's OK." Janice tried to reassure Lora, without really knowing how Emma was. "Who hurt you baby?"

"Oh, Mommy." Lora paused. Janice looked at David and nodded towards the door.

"I'll just go talk to the police and tell them you would like to speak to them, honey." David looked at Janice, sadly, and left the room. He wanted to give them a few minutes alone before bringing in the police woman who was waiting outside.

"Can you tell the police who did this?" Janice asked Lora, again.

"I was so scared." Lora cried.

"I know, but you're safe now. We have to get the person who did this so he doesn't hurt anyone else. Do you understand that?" Janice was holding Lora's hand to her lips. "There is a very nice police woman just outside who wants to ask you a few questions. Just tell her what you can, baby. I know it's difficult."

"I don't know his name. I never saw him before." Lora was sobbing softly.

The police woman tapped lightly on the door and entered. "Hi Lora, I am Detective Olivia Marks. Could I talk to you for a few minutes? It's OK for your mother to stay with you." Olivia was five foot tall with short brown hair. She was twenty-five, but looked and sounded much younger, which was probably an asset when questioning young victims such as Lora.

Lora simply nodded her head and held onto her mother's hand tightly. She didn't look at the detective. She kept her gaze down, in shame. She couldn't look at her mother either.

"Do you know who hurt you and your friend?"

Lora shook her head "no." After a pause she said, "He said his friends called him 'Smilin' Jack.' I never saw him before." Lora spoke so softly that the detective had to strain to hear her. She jotted the information in her small notebook as she listened.

"Can you describe him for me? Hair, eyes, height, and age, anything you can remember?"

Lora looked up at the detective for the first time. It was a brief curious glance. She wondered what the person behind the voice looked like, then looked down at her blanket. "He was tall. About twenty, or so, I guess. He said he was in college."

When no more information followed Olivia asked, "And his hair and eyes?"

"Short, blond hair. Dark sunglasses." She kept her answers brief.

"Did he take off the glasses at any point?"

"Yes." Lora paused. "His eyes." Another pause.

"Yes, what about his eyes?"

"They were the most unusual shade of blue." It was as if Lora was seeing them, again. She pushed the palm of her hand into her closed eye. The other was all ready swollen shut and sore.

"I'm sorry, Lora but can you be more specific?" Olivia was trying to be patient. She saw Janice reach for Lora's hand.

"You're safe now, baby. Please talk to the detective." Janice brushed the side of Lora's tear stained cheek with the back of her other hand. Tears were falling down her own face, as she watched her tortured daughter reliving her nightmare.

"They were so light, and cold, like ice." Lora finally volunteered.

"What was he wearing?" Olivia looked to Janice and gave her a reassuring look. "You're doing very well, here, Lora."

"Cut-off jeans and brown sandals."

"That's very good. Anything else like a tattoo or scar that you can remember? Anything distinguishing would help." Olivia wrote in her book, as she asked the question, and looked at Lora , awaiting an answer.

Lora thought for a moment. "He was carrying a cooler of beer, and a camera bag. I really can't remember anything else. Please I don't want to talk about this anymore." Tears started falling again.

"OK, Hun, That's fine. You've been very helpful. If you do think of anything your mother can call me." Olivia closed her notebook and looked at Janice. " Thank you both. I'll be in touch." She then left the room.

David had been to Emma's room. He talked with her parents, who were standing outside of her door. The doctor was with Emma. They told David that she had a slight concussion, but had not been raped. *Thank you for that,* he thought. He spoke with Emma's parents for a few more minutes; then returned to his daughter's room to find the detective exiting. David was waiting by the door, just outside the room. "Well, who did this to our girls?" He was mad, as he was concerned.

"She didn't have much for a name, but gave a pretty good description. Now, let me get to work on it. If Lora remembers anything else give me a call." Olivia gave him her card. "I'm going to see if the other girl can add anything."

"I hope you catch the bastard, Excuse my language. I have to go to my family, now." David went into the room and straight to his daughter's bed. Detective Marks went to Emma's room. Emma had regained consciousness and was able to give the same description as Lora. Emma was very upset about what had happened to her friend. She wanted to go to her, but no one would let her get out of bed. Emma felt responsible, because she felt she had encouraged the guy.

Lora and Emma spent the night in the hospital. The next day they were released, and each went to their homes without speaking. It would be a week before Emma was able to call Lora to check on her. She was so relieved to hear her friend's voice. "I have been so worried about you, Lora. I'm so sorry. I never should have talked to the stranger."

"Emma, it isn't your fault. I don't blame you. You couldn't have known that creep was so sick." Lora still was sore and black and blue. "How's your head? My dad said you had a concussion."

"Yeah, but the headaches have gotten better. May I come over and see you?"

"You'd better have your mother call mine. She's staying pretty close to me and the house, these days."

"My mother won't let me out of her sight either. I think it would be good for our mom's to visit with each other, too."

Emma's mother brought Emma to visit with Lora while she visited with Janice. Lora and Emma didn't talk about the incident at the pond. It was still too fresh and painful. It was just comforting to see each other. They began to form a special bond, a bond that would continue to grow over the rest of the summer. Lora never went away to camp in August, as planned. She had no interest in going away. She couldn't even bring herself to go to Emma's. Emma's mother would drive her to visit with Lora almost every day. The girls had sleepovers at Lora's, where the girls watched movies and listened to music. Always, the music made Lora feel better. She began to write some songs of her own. She spent hours at the piano. The only one that she shared them with, was Emma.

Chapter Two
The Aftermath

Lora continued to meet with a rape crisis counselor, once a week, throughout the summer. She was making real progress. Emma would stop by to visit almost every day. The girls sang, watched movies, and kept each other company. They had grown closer through their joint experience. By the middle of August, the girls were talking about going shopping for back-to-school clothes, and getting excited about the idea of returning to school. Their parents were so happy to see some joy and excitement returning to their lives.

Then, one morning, Lora woke up ill. A new nightmare was about to alter her plans. Terrified yet another time this summer, she called her mother, who was back working part time. When her mother heard her daughter's symptoms, she was horrified for her. "Not this!" Janice called her OBGYN and made an appointment for Lora, for that afternoon. She wouldn't call David until she knew more.

Lora and Janice sat in the car, after the doctor visit, not speaking. Neither one knew what to say or do. Their worst fear had been confirmed by the doctor. "Mom, what am I going to do?" Lora broke down and cried.

"I don't know Sweetie, but we will figure this out, together." Janice reached over to hug Lora. Your dad and I are right here with you. You don't have to face this alone.

"I'm scared." Lora cried on her mother's shoulder.

"I know. I'm scared, too." Janice was as to how this, too, would change her daughter's life forever. She always believed that God doesn't give you more than you can handle. But all this was too much. How could her little girl cope?

The Logan's were a devout Catholic family. They didn't believe in abortion, but they never dreamed that they would be in this position, either. In the days following the devastating news, the Logan's met with their priest and had intense discussions among themselves to decide what would be the best solution for everyone. They discussed adoption, of course, but in the end, Lora insisted on keeping the baby. Her parents decided that they would raise the child as their own, in the public eye, in order to protect Lora's reputation and her future. They put their house on the market, and David began looking for employment out of state. Lora was devastated to be leaving her friends, especially Emma. No one knew about the incident. Emma hadn't told anyone; it was a private horror the girls and their families kept to themselves.

Janice was able to sell the house, quickly. David found a job with a construction company in Arizona. David went out to start his job and to find a new home for his family. Janice stayed behind to close on their home, and prepare for the move. David found a lovely ranch, on several acres, and Janice and Lora flew out to check it out. Everyone fell in love with it and its seclusion. It was an "L" shaped house with a huge front porch. Lora would be home schooled for the next year. Everything was falling into place. Emma would fly out, on school vacation, to visit, which would help make the adjustment more bearable for the girls.,

Detective Marks kept the family updated on the investigation, but the attacker had not been apprehended, and the leads were growing cold. She apologized, but reassured them she was staying on the case. She had grown very close to the families and stopped by often to see Lora. She encouraged Lora to continue with her music. Lora promised her that she would. It was her only true sanctuary and escape from her nightmare. When she was singing she was at peace, and spent hours at her piano every day. No longer were all of her songs sad.

Every morning that she felt sick was a reminder of what had happened, and what will be. Lora was frightened, and her mother knew it. Janice tried to reassure her and be supportive of the mature decisions Lora had made. She was very proud of her daughter and the way she was handling everything. She was still a child, though, and Janice was her mother. Janice cried in her room at night. She had failed to protect her child and blamed herself for all that had happened. Of course, David told her that it wasn't her fault. There was no way anyone could have known this would happen. He would hold her, stroke her hair, and comfort her. David would go to his daughter's room, after his wife fell asleep, look down at his restless sleeping child, and cry. He prayed for her and for his family to heal. He prayed for the strength and wisdom to care for them.

The move went smoothly. David made arrangements, at his end, for the move. Janice stayed to see that the movers packed everything and followed the moving van in her car, with Lora. Of course there was a tearful goodbye with Emma and her family, and promises to call and visit often.

When they were under way, Lora put on her headphones to her MP3 player. She sat watching the only world she had known, slowly disappear, and lost herself in the music. Janice let Lora have her time and space. They rode without speaking for the first hour. They stopped for lunch at a small roadside diner. Surrounded by strangers they felt comfortable for the first time in months. They even joked with each other. It was almost like nothing had ever happened, if only for a short time. Reality always found its way back to the forefront of their lives.

The road trip went smoothly. Lora called Emma on her cell phone several times. They got to their new home before the moving van. David was there to greet them. They spent the first night in their new home sleeping on the floor. The electricity was on, but they chose to use candles for lighting for a little adventure.

When the moving van finally arrived the next day, Janice and David were kept busy giving the movers directions. Lora explored outside her new home. They had twenty acres of open fields, forest, and a creek that ran through it. The house was set way back from the main road to Flagstaff. Lora looked down the two-hundred-foot driveway to the main road. This was very private and peaceful. For the first time in months, Lora felt safe. She took a deep breath of the brisk autumn air. She began to sing softly, when she felt the baby move for the first time. The little flutter inside her belly startled her. She stopped singing, abruptly, and put her hand to her still flat stomach. She began to sing again, and the baby moved once more, bringing a smile to Lora's face. "We're home baby." She spoke to her unborn child often after that day.

That night she shared the experience with her mother. The whole impending, surreal birth was now a reality. Lora's swelling abdomen was additional evidence that all of their lives were about to change. It was hard for Janice to be excited about the birth of her first grandchild. On the other hand, all life was sacred, and a gift from God. This baby would be loved, for how could they not love her. They had learned that the child would be a girl. Lora began to consider names for her daughter; a daughter that would be her sister to the rest of the world.

The Logan's settled into their new home and new lives. Lora was home schooled by her mother and continued to practice her piano. David was doing well with his new company and received several promotions. He was now site manager on a large project, which was most welcome, since Janice wasn't able to work, right now. Lora roamed around the property, but only left the ranch for doctor appointments. She didn't mind. She still had a fear of leaving her home. The ranch was so peaceful and relaxing. She threw herself into her school work and was excelling. She would be able to skip a grade in school. When she enrolled next fall she would enter eleventh grade. She was making plans to attend Northern Arizona University, after graduation. Her parents encouraged her to plan for her future. They wanted her to experience as much of a normal youth as possible, after the birth.

They wanted her to dream, and dream she did. Lora dreamed of proms and graduation. She dreamed of college. She dreamed of music and making a career of it, somehow. The one thing she never dreamed about was dating. She still was experiencing night mares. The thought of being close to a guy was terrifying. She saw *his* eyes in her dreams and heard *his* voice in her ears whenever it was dark and quiet.

The winter passed, and with it, the holidays. Emma came on winter break and spent some time with Lora, which was welcome in her isolated world. She was able to be a teen, if only for a time.

After the first of the year, Lora grew very quiet and stayed in her room, most of the time. Her mother knew she was anxious, but wasn't successful in abating her daughter's fears.

Finally, during a snowy March day, the contractions began. Janice called her husband and the doctor. David came home to drive his family to the hospital, where the doctor was waiting for them. At 3:45 PM, Tuesday March 5, 1998, Melodie Grace Logan was born. She was a tiny 5lbs 6ozs and had a full head of dark hair. She looked just like her mother, except for the light blue eyes. How could God be so cruel as to give her *his* eyes. It didn't take Lora long to overcome looking into these warm blue eyes. These eyes that soon filled with love, and melted her cold heart.

Lora and the baby stayed in the hospital for twenty-four hours, then David took them both home. The Logan family began their new life together. They slowly made their way into the community, where they had lived for the past seven months in isolation. They joined a church and had the baby baptized. Lora began piano lessons and even found a voice teacher. She continued to be home schooled and decided to finish out her high school at home. She planned to apply to the university in the fall of 2000. Lora joined a summer theater group and got a summer job in a little shop on Main street. She got her driver's license and made a couple of friends at work. She didn't date. She spent as much time as she could with her little girl, whom she loved with all her heart. She didn't know she was capable of so much love. Melodie had the sweetest personality. She smiled and giggled all the time. She was so playful, and hardly ever complained, or whined. She was curious and learned to walk early. Janice and David doted on this tiny version of Lora. Janice stayed home to care for Melodie, while Lora went to work and took classes at the college. Lora had decided to become a music teacher, but never gave up her dream of becoming a performer. She loved to write music and sang her songs to her little girl, who was her best fan. She always applauded for her mother, whom she called 'Mimi.'

Chapter Three
The Dream
May 2004

*L*ora was completing her last year of college when she saw the advertisement for auditions, being held in Phoenix. It was for a new Celebrity USA contest. It was a new TV reality show for want-to-be singing talent. The winner won a hundred-thousand dollars and a recording contract. She decided then, that this is what she wanted. At dinner that night she brought it up with her parents. "I have to go to Phoenix next week Mom."

"What for, Lora?"

"They're holding auditions for that new show, *Celebrity USA*. I really want to try out. I think I have a good chance of getting on the show."

"It sounds really exciting. Maybe we can make a shopping trip out of it." Janice still found it hard to let Lora go far, alone. She didn't know if she would ever get over her feelings of guilt for not being there when her daughter needed her most. She had even seen a therapist, but she still couldn't get over it. She grew very protective of Melodie, too.

"Yeah, that sounds great, Mom. Doesn't that sound like fun, Mel? Maybe we can get a few outfits for summer."

"Are we going to sleep there, Mimi?" Melodie had called Lora "Mimi", instead of mommy, since she was old enough to speak. It helped avoid any embarrassing slips that might have occurred in public. Some day she would learn the truth of the circumstances of her birth, but at age six she was still too young to understand. Janice was momma and Lora remained Mimi. Melodie would be entering first grade, in the fall, and was very excited about that.

"Yes Mel, I am going to sing for some people." Lora explained to her daughter. "If they like my singing enough, I'ill be able to sing in a contest to decide who the best is."

"Mimi, you are the best. I all ready know that." Melodie continued to eat her dinner.

"Well thank you, sweetheart. Let's hope the judges agree with you." Lora winked at her mother.

"You're very talented, Lora. I really think you have a genuine shot at this. Don't you, David?"

"No question you can sing with the best of them, baby." David smiled at Lora. "Are you sure you're up for this?" He was referring to her emotional health. It was far from home, and there would be crowds.

Lora knew to what her father was inferring. "It's what I have been dreaming of my whole life; to sing for someone and be *discovered*. I want to be an entertainer," she said, a bit starry eyed.

"Then I say go for it!" Lora hopped from her chair and gave her dad a hug around his-neck. "Hey! hungry man eating here." He laughed at her excitement.

"Melodie and I will be there to cheer you on," Janice said, as Lora rushed to give her a hug, too.

"I have to call Emma. She'll be thrilled!" Lora ran off to her room to make her call.

David and Janice exchanged knowing glances. Would they ever get over their protectiveness of their daughter? "I'll be with her," Janice said. David gave a slight nod of understanding.

The whole week was a whirlwind of activity. Reservations had to be made at the Point South Mountain Resort. Lora went shopping for the perfect outfit. Songs had to be picked out and practiced. Lora practiced in front of a mirror, like she did when she was little, with her hairbrush in her hand. Melodie thought it was all so much fun. Lora had her hair and nails done the Friday before they left. She had to be in line Saturday morning to get a wristband which would allow her access to the performer's line. It would be a grueling couple of days, just waiting to get in if she could.

The hotel was packed with starry eyed people, all wanting a chance to show their stuff.

Lora was a bit overwhelmed, having been living a rather quiet, unassuming life. Melodie, on the other hand, was savoring every minute. She had always been quiet a forward and precocious little girl. She was always center stage if there was an audience; a born performer, like her mother.

"Mimi, I want to sing for the judges, too," the seven year old announced.

"Not this time, Mel. Now hold our hands, and don't let go. You don't want to get lost in all these people." Lora held onto her daughters hand a little too tightly.

"Mimi, you're squeezing me!"

"Oh, I'm sorry. I didn't mean to. I just don't want you to get lost." Lora and Janice finally reached the check-in desk and gave their name. The woman welcomed them and handed them a key card to their room. She wished Lora good luck in the contest, when she learned of the reason for their visit, from Melodie.

Lora was so happy to finally arrive at their door. The three were sharing a room with two double beds. Lora set her suitcase down on a table, at the foot of one of the beds, closest to the heavily draped window. Melodie ran to look out of the window. She pulled the drapes apart and disappeared behind them. They were several floors above ground and had a great view of the city, once Lora pulled the drapes to each side to reveal it. Melodie ran into the bathroom and squealed upon discovering all the little soaps and shampoos in there. She thought they were hers and had been made just for her. "Look Mimi, just my size!" They looked much bigger in her small hands.

"Wow! Mel. Aren't they nice? They must have known you were coming." Lora was taking her dress from her suitcase and hanging it in the closet. "Mimi has to hurry and get her wristband. You be a good girl, and stay with momma. We can go get some dinner when I get back." She kissed Melodie and said "Wish Mimi luck, baby."

"OK, Mimi. A kiss for luck," She gave Lora a big hug around her neck and kissed her lips with a smack.

"OOOh I love you so much, Melodie." She hugged Melodie back, and then stood and turned to her mother.

Janice gave her a hug and kiss. "Good luck, honey."

"Thanks Mom. I'd better get going. Have fun you two. I'm so glad you're here with me."

Lora left to find the line to get a wristband. She was excited as she followed the signs that led her to a line in front of a set of huge double wooden doors, with shiny brass handles. There were several desks, set in a row, in the red carpeted hallway. Lora stood in line for the table that had the letters J-P on a sign hanging above it. The line was moving slowly, but everyone was friendly and cordial. She enjoyed chatting with the people who were in line near her. They were as hopeful as she was. When she finally made her way to the desk, she filled out a short form and got a bright pink, rubber wristband. She was one step closer to her dream. She sighed as she put it on. Her heart beat a little faster with excitement. She had been instructed to return the next morning at 9 AM, wearing the newly acquired wristband, to participate in the first round of auditions. Lora practically floated to her room. When she got to her door, she opened it only slightly and waved her wristband arm into the room. Her mother and daughter applauded, and Melodie squealed with delight.

"That was the easy part. I have to be back at 9 AM for the first audition. Let's go get some dinner and relax the rest of the night." She picked up Melodie and spun her around. "We can have a pajama party and watch a movie. How does that sound, baby?"

"Yeah! Can we have pizza for dinner?"

Janice said she had been looking at the room service menu. "They really offer a wide variety. What would you like Lora? We can eat right here."

"Oh that sounds perfect. I'm really tired of the crowds. I think I'd like something light. How about a Greek salad?"

"I'll call down, and you two can get into your PJ's." Janice picked up the phone, while the girls went into the bathroom. Melodie was only too happy to wash up, using the new, personal sized soap.

Lora got Melodie ready for bed, and then herself. She sat on the bed in her cotton, sleeveless nightgown, put Melodie in front of her, and began to brush her long, dark, wavy hair, just like her mother use to do for her. Janice looked at them and smiled to herself. They really were beautiful girls. Lora was singing softly as she brushed.

It was only "You Are My Sunshine" but she sang it beautifully, and Melodie was singing with her. It was such a touching moment, it brought tears to Janice's eyes. Janice prayed for only the best in both of the girls' lives. She knew how quickly things can change, though, and sometimes, without any warning.

There came a knock on the door. Janice opened the door to a bell hop, who rolled in a cart covered with a white cloth, with several covered dishes. Janice gave the man a tip and thanked him. "Thank you and good evening ladies" he said, as he left pulling the door closed after him.

Lora put Melodies hair in a single braid for the night. Janice removed the covers from the dishes.

"My pizza!" Melodie bounced off the bed and skipped over to the cart. "It smells so good!" She was rubbing her hands together in excited anticipation.

"Here, Mel. You sit up here, and I 'll get you a piece." Lora folded the coverlet back and spread out a towel for Melody to sit on. She placed a plate down in front of her and began to cut a piece of pizza into smaller pieces, in hopes the child would make less of a mess. Then she stacked the pillows up against the headboard and sat, leaned against them, with her bowl of salad. "Hurry up mom, Melodie is going to eat all of the pizza."

Janice called from the bathroom, "She better leave me a piece." Janice emerged from the bathroom in a hotel white, terrycloth robe and turned on the TV. "Let's see what movie we have here." Janice began to scan through the options. "Look! *'Brother Bear'*, I like that one."

"That sounds good to me, Lora said. How about you, Mel?"

"MMM. This is the best pizza I ever had."

"You say that about every pizza you eat. Now, what about the movie?" Lora wiped Melodie's mouth with a napkin.

"OK, I love that one. Can I have another piece and a drink, please?"

"May I?" Lora corrected. "Yes you may have another slice." Lora prepared another slice for Melodie and got her a glass of milk from the cart. Janice started the movie and helped herself to some pizza. Melodie fell asleep before the end of the movie, and Lora tucked her under the covers. "I think I'll turn in, too, Mom. I don't know how much sleep I'm going to get. I'm so nervous."

"You'll be fine. Once you start singing, you will be one with the music. You know how you are."

"Thanks mom. I love you."

"I love you, too, honey. Now get some rest, Lora, I'm so proud of you."

Lora tossed and turned all night, partly because Melodie hogged most of the bed by positioning her body horizontally across it. Lora got up early and was showered and dressed when Melodie awoke.

"I'm hungry." Melodie had barely opened her eyes and was looking for breakfast.

"I all ready called down for some food. Now, go wash up, honey." There was a light knock on the door. Lora looked out to see the bellhop with the breakfast cart. She let him in and tipped him. Janice stirred in her bed.

"Is that coffee I smell?" She asked, yawning and stretching.

"Yes mom, just a little continental breakfast, with pancakes for Mel."

"Did you say pancakes?" Melodie burst into the room from the bathroom. "Oh boy!"

Lora had a little juice. She was too nervous to eat. "Well, you two have fun, today. I'm going to head on down."

"OK, sweetheart. We'll be down a little later." Janice removed the lid from Melodie's pancakes and helped her sit at the table, in the corner, to eat.

It only took four hours to be called to sing. Lora waited with all the other performers. They would be called to enter through the wooden double doors, emerging either in tears or waving a paper that invited them to the next round of auditions. Lora got the paper. Her mother and Melodie were waiting outside the doors with other contestants and their families. Lora held the paper high over her head and screamed " I'M GOING TO HOLLYWOOD!" Lora was jumping up and down with excitement, like a little girl at Christmas.

Melodie ran to her and tried to grab her bouncing legs. "I'm going, too!"

Janice joined in the excitement of the moment. "I knew you could do it!" She grabbed her bouncing daughter and bounced along with her and Melodie. "We are going to Hollywood!" They said it over and over, as if to make it sink in.

"I have to call Emma! She is going to die!" Lora took out her cell phone and called Emma. There was much screaming and unintelligible, fast spoken words, but Lora and Emma knew what each other was saying.

"I take it she's thrilled for you?" Her mother asked.

Lora closed her cell phone. "Oh yes, very." Lora was grinning ear to ear.

"I think there's someone else you should call." Janice suggested.

"Yes, Daddy will be so happy." Lora opened her phone again to call her father. The phone rang several times before he answered. "I DID IT! I AM GOING TO HOLLYWOOD!"

Janice couldn't hear her husband's end of the conversation, but could imagine what he was saying by the big smile on Lora's face. She also knew what he was thinking because she was thinking the same things. She hoped it didn't show on her face. She kept smiling, all the while feeling anxious, but thrilled for Lora.

"So. What's next?" Janice asked Lora, when she was through speaking to her father.

"They told me to take this to the registration desk and pick up an envelope with further instructions and dates."

"Then we had better go pick that up."

"And then can we go shopping Mimi? I want a new dress."

"We'll definitely do some shopping and celebrating!" Janice smoothed Melodies hair back from her smiling face. "How does that sound?"

"HORRAY!" Melodie started jumping and tugging at Janice's hand.

"OK. Lora has to go do something. Let's meet in the lobby in say … fifteen minutes?" Janice looked at Lora for confirmation.

"Yes, that sounds good." Lora headed for the registration desk on the second floor. Janice took Melodie back to the room to have a snack and to use the bathroom. Janice called the Rokerij and made reservations for dinner at 7 PM. She had heard it was one of the best places to eat, in Phoenix.

The three arrived in the lobby at exactly the same time. They spent the rest of the afternoon shopping at the Metro Center Mall and spent a little time at the Phoenix Zoo. They arrived at the Rokerij just before 7 PM. They were in luck, their table was ready. They went upstairs to the formal dining-room. The tables were draped with crisp, white linen and the room was lit with glistening candles. Janice wanted someplace special, befitting their celebration. They enjoyed their steak and seafood dinners, but were so exhausted they went back to the hotel and to bed. The next day they drove back home.

The next round of competitions would be in Hollywood, in August. Depending on how well Lora did, she would be there two days to four weeks. That gave her a month to prepare and make all the arrangements. Janice helped in any way she could. She booked a room at the Comfort Inn and Suites. They served a free continental breakfast, daily, which would help with expenses. It was close to the NBC studios, in case Lora went all the way in the contest.

Lora spent her time gathering sheet music and practicing. She knew she would have to have a wide variety of songs. Emma flew out for two weeks to help Lora prepare. She gave Lora encouragement and moral support. She distracted Lora at times in order to help her relax and have some fun with Melodie. Emma had to leave to return to her job. Until she graduated from the local community college, that May, she worked part time at the local battered women's shelter. She was now working full time as a social worker. She loved both the work and the people.

Emma knew how important this contest was to Lora. Lora confided things in Emma that she didn't share with her parents. Lora's parents had been so over-protective, since the attack that Lora felt smothered at times. She needed this for her self esteem and to feel some sort of normalcy in her life. Becoming a mother at fifteen was not her plan. Now she was twenty-one with, a seven year old child. As much as Lora loved Melodie, she secretly wanted more. Lora wanted her life to mean something. Her whole life was centered around her family. She wanted to stand apart from them; to do something on her own. She wanted her daughter to be proud of her. She wanted to be proud of herself.

CELEBRITY

As much as Emma loved her parents, she was secretly happy when they decided to leave New York in favor of the warmer Miami winters. She, too, felt suffocated. Even during her years at college, her parents had insisted she live at home. Now they worried all the time, since she had decided to move to the "big city". Emma actually enjoyed it there. She enjoyed her work and, outside of her job, her autonomy. She didn't have many friends, other than Lora. She hadn't had a meaningful relationship with a man; although, she did date. Her life was full and she was happy. She wanted that for Lora and hoped this contest would bring that to her life.

Chapter Four
Reach for the Stars
August 2004

*L*ora's father decided to take two-week's vacation and drive to Hollywood with his family. They would spend the whole two weeks on vacation there, no matter what happened with the contest. They settled into their rooms at the Comfort Inn and did a little sight-seeing before dinner. Lora was scheduled to perform the next day, at 10 AM. She would have two minutes to impress the judges. She chose "Candle in the Wind" because it had, for years, been one of her favorites, and she was so familiar with it. It was comfortable for her.

The family donned their NBC pass necklaces and left for the studio just around the corner. Everyone was so excited. They were directed to the studio on the lot, where the auditions were being held. They found hundreds of people milling around, outside of the studio. Some had brought lawn chairs, and it was a real party atmosphere. The exhilaration in the air was almost smothering. None of the Logan's had experienced anything like this. Lora did a good job of staying focused. She wanted this more than anything in her life.

It was a way of feeling the self-worth, which she had been seeking since she was fourteen, that had been taken from her in a single afternoon. Her self-worth and her childhood had come to an abrupt end that summer day. Even though she tried not to think about it, it was part of her everyday life. And her daughter, with her ice blue color eyes, was a constant reminder.

Lora's name was called. Her parents wished her luck, as she hurried for the studio door. She turned and gave a final little wave as she entered. She sang her heart out for the judges. They even let her sing more of the song than she had expected to sing. They were speechless for a moment. They just starred. Lora was worried. Then the first judge shook his head and began to applaud. The next thing she knew all three judges were applauding her.

The female judge had a glistening to her eyes. "You are going to go far in this competition, young lady." The other judges nodded in agreement. "We look forward to hearing more from you. This is the best we have heard today."

"Thank you so much." Lora spoke so softly in comparison to the song she had just sung. She couldn't wait to tell her parents.

Lora's call backs continued, and David had to return to work. He promised to be watching on TV. He was beginning to feel better about the contest. Lora was performing brilliantly and was working with hair and make-up specialists. The songs had a bit of choreographing to them. And she was working with professional musicians who were very helpful. Each new performance was a challenge, and Lora was up for each one.

As the contestants were eliminated one by one, the world became more focused on the remaining few. Who would become the new Celebrity USA? The media was following the few remaining contestants, and interviews were becoming daily occurrences. The public wanted to know everything about these talented, up-and-coming stars. Janice was very careful about keeping Melodie out of the spot light and away from cameras. It was no easy task with the outgoing youngster. She loved the cameras and people following them everywhere. Janice even considered sending Melodie home, to be away from it all. Lora couldn't bear to be away from her just now.

The contest was now down to three singers. Brian, a twelve year old who could sing and dance like Michael Jackson. Nichole, a Gothic looking performer, always in a black costume, black make-up, and long painted, black nails. Lora took a liking to her, though, and they became good friends. Nichole was ten years her senior, and it was obvious that she knew her way around a stage. She had been singing in clubs for several years. She came off as a hard-ass bitch, but she was one of the most kind and gentle people Lora had ever met. They promised to remain friends no matter how the contest turned out. Lora told Emma all about her, and when Emma flew out to stay with Lora, for the end of the contest, all three girls became the best of friends. It was like high school should have been, but never was, for Lora.

The final night of the contest arrived at last. Brian had been voted out the night before. The girls were told to sing a Beatles song. They could choose which one. Nichole chose the fast-paced, "Rock and Roll Music", where she played her electric guitar and was spectacular. The crowd gave her a standing ovation. Lora chose, "The Long and Winding Road", which to her, symbolized her life , up until this moment. She began seated–at her piano, and as she got further into the song, she stood and went towards the audience. They were mesmerized by the emotion and feeling she put into the song. Even the judges stood at the end. Janice and David were in the audience. Emma was watching from the hotel room with Melodie. At the end of her performance they had tears in their eyes. Lora did it. She sang her heart out for the people, and they loved her.

All that was left was for the people to vote. They would return tomorrow night for the result. The ten finalists were going to put on a finale show preceding the announcement of the winner. Lora's nerves were raw. She was exhausted and exhilarated at the same time. She had to fight her way through a throng of new fans and media. This was still new to her. She was thankful to see her parents across the room. Lora made her way towards them, and they wrapped her in their arms.

"That was awesome Lora!" Emma had called Lora's cell phone.

"It really was, honey!" Janice exclaimed, just before kissing her cheek.

David wrapped his arm around her shoulder to shield her from the crowd. "Let's get out of here." He guided the women towards the exit. "Please, no more questions." He told the media. Flash bulbs continued to illuminate the area and followed them, as they made their way out of the building. They were bombarded with questions. David tried to hurry the woman along, but it was slow going in the multitude of fans. The crowd followed them all the way to their car. David let the women in and told them to lock their doors. He went around and got in the driver's side. He drove slowly, at first, until he cleared most of the people. He didn't drive right to the hotel. He wasn't ready to meet up with another mob, so soon. He drove to the Gibson Amphitheater, so they all could regroup and catch their breath. They got out of the car and walked around.

"Have you thought about what you'll do if you win, sweetheart?" David walked with his arm around Lora.

"I haven't thought about anything else."

"Your life will get very hectic for awhile. This crowd tonight is just the beginning."

"A recording contract Dad! Me on a CD, radio, music video, TV, even a tour," This is all surreal.

"And you're all right with this?"

"I'd like the chance to find out Daddy."

David kissed her forehead, "Then, I hope your dream comes true, tomorrow. Just remember your mother and I will always be there for you. We're so proud of you, no matter what happens tomorrow night." David was holding her face in his hands like he did when she was a child. "Promise me you won't lose who you are. I love this young woman that you have become." He kissed her cheek. "You've come a long way, sweet heart."

"I promise, Daddy. I love you." She kissed him and gave him a hug, laying her head on his strong shoulder.

"Well, we'd better get to the hotel. This new super star needs her beauty rest."

Janice came to Lora's side and slipped her arm in Lora's. The two women, giggling, walked to the car, side by side. Janice slipped her arm into David's as he walked along. Janice looked up at him. "She has a good head on her shoulders, David. She can handle herself."

"It's not her I worry about, so much. It's how others treat her that concerns me." Janice laid her head on David's shoulder as they walked to the car.

Lora was busy most of the day, with rehearsal, wardrobe, and make-up. It kept her too busy to dwell on the contest results. Before she knew it, she was on stage with Nicole, holding her breath, and Nichole's hand.

"THE WINNER OF CELEBRITY USA IS..." the pause was only seconds but it felt like hours. "LORA LOGAN!" Lora and Nichole hugged each other. Nicole whispered, "Congratulations."

Nichole was truly happy for Lora. Nichole was going to do well. She had an agent, now, and there were deals in the works. The hard part would be keeping in touch with their new crazy lives.

There was a wrap-up party for the reality show, and it went well into the night, and, until early the next morning. Janice, David, and Lora left early. Emma was waiting at the hotel with the sleeping Melodie. They had their own private celebration at 10 O'clock when they arrived with pizza and beer. The stress of competing was over. Tonight was for letting her hair down and kicking back with family and her closest friend. Lora had invited Nichole to come back with them, but she was enjoying the party and opted to stay there. They hugged and promised to see each other the next day.

Back in the Logan's room, the barefoot, bathrobe clad Lora was curled up in an overstuffed chair with a slice of pizza balancing in her two hands. Emma was seated on the floor with her back to the chair Lora was sitting in. Janice and David were seated on the sofa across from Lora's chair. Melodie was asleep in the bed.

"Well, Miss hot shot celebrity!" David was smiling when he said it. "What happens next?"

"I have a meeting with the shows' producer to collect my prize money! Then I have to meet with the record producer. I have a photo shoot, lunch with a potential agent, and Emma and I wanted to see the *Hollywood Walk of Fame,* before we have to leave." Lora took a sip of beer

"I have phoned my lawyer back home. We need to set up a

meeting with him as soon as we can. I want your rights protected. Don't sign anything unless he looks at it, promise?"

"Thanks Dad. You and mom have been so supportive and helpful. All this is because of you. I couldn't have done this without you. I love you both so much!"

Janice went over to sit next to Lora, "Your father and I only want the best for you. I hope this is what you truly want. We want you to be happy."

"I am so happy right now. That's all I ever wanted to do was to sing and make people feel happy."

Emma wiped her mouth on a napkin and reached for another slice of pizza. "Well you certainly accomplished that with that last song you sang. I started dialing in my vote, then and there."

"Hey, I want pizza too." Melodie was sitting up on the bed rubbing her right eye with her hand.

"We're sorry. Did we wake you?" Lora went to her daughter and sat beside her to give her a hug. "I have some exciting news. I won the contest!"

"Are you famous, now?" Melodie asked.

"Well, yes I guess I am a little famous. A lot of people watch that show, and many of them voted for me to win."

"Does that mean you can't live with momma, and poppa, and me?"

Lora kissed Melodie on the head. "We'll still be a family. I'll have to travel and be away, sometimes, though." Then with an excited voice she told Melodie, "I'm going to make a CD, and they'll play my songs on the radio! Won't that be special?"

"But I'll miss you when you are gone"

"And I'll miss you, too, so much. But you'll be able to go with me, sometimes. It will be an adventure," Lora reassured her.

Chapter Five
The Adventure Begins
Fall 2004

*L*ife at the Logan's had returned to some sort of normalcy. Melodie had started First grade, and Lora and Janice had watched her drive away in a big, yellow school bus that seemed to swallow her up. David worked long hours, but never failed to make it home for dinner. Janice was working for her state real estate license, for the state of Arizona. She wanted to work part time, again, now that Melodie was in school all day.

Lora had found an agent that she really liked. Molly McDonald was a small town girl, at heart, although she grew up in San Francisco. She was four-foot, eleven, with fire red hair; a small bundle of energy. Molly understood that Lora wanted to avoid a lot of the publicity, although she didn't know why. Lora used her family as an excuse, but didn't go into details. Lora knew she had to do a certain amount of promotional work in order to sell her CDs. Molly arranged for a back-up band and booked Lora on a few national talk shows to get her "feet wet" with the media. Her father's lawyer checked every contract and kept an eye on the publicist assigned to Lora. He had final approval over anything that was going to be published about Lora and her family. He recommended a financial advisor that Lora's father hired to help keep Lora's new found financial affairs in order. It was all very overwhelming and consuming, but things soon began running smoothly. Lora Logan was becoming a business.

Lora's first public appearance, after winning the contest, was in New York City. She made an appearance on a morning news show and several talk shows. Her appearances consisted of singing a song and answering a couple of questions. She was treated like royalty, by the shows. The paparazzi followed her everywhere, snapping pictures, and calling her name. She wasn't fond of that, but Molly was with her all the time and guided her through the maze of cameras. The shows provided her with airfare, and a car to pick her up and chauffeur her around. They did her hair and make-up at each appearance. It was Molly's job, after all, to see that Lora's career got off to a good start. Everything was moving very fast. Molly directed Lora to some shops, in New York, where she might find some outfits in which to perform. She made suggestions, but was never pushy. She knew Lora wanted to be true to herself, first and foremost. She wasn't going to change who she was to please others.

After their weekend on the New York shows, Molly returned to her office in the city to arrange for Lora's recording session. Lora flew to Albany, where Emma met her for a day together. Lora needed to unwind with a friendly face, for awhile. Emma took Lora to her apartment, and they had a quiet dinner. They talked about everything that was happening in Lora's life. The next morning Emma took Lora to the airport for her return flight to Arizona. Luckily, few paparazzi hung out at the Albany airport. Lora was able to board her plane without making a scene. Her mother and Melodie were waiting for her at the Flagstaff, Pulliam Airport. It felt good to be home. No paparazzi to greet her there, either. They walked to the baggage claim and collected her bag. One young woman, about Lora's age, recognized her and asked for her autograph. Lora was delighted to oblige her. Of course, Melodie was full of questions.

"Why did that lady want you to write for her? Why were you gone so long? When is Molly coming to visit?" The questions continued during most of the ride home. Lora didn't really mind. She had missed Melodie wholeheartedly. This was going to be the worst part of all this, leaving her daughter.

"Let's stop and pick up some Chinese take-out, for dinner." Lora suggested, knowing it was one of Melodies favorite meals.

"OOH, sweet and sour chicken and egg rolls?"

"Sounds good to me! How about you, momma?"

"Anything that doesn't involve cooking, sounds good to me," Janice teased.

The girls picked up the take-out, and were driving down the road to their house, when they saw several vehicles parked on the side of the road across from their drive. As they drove nearer, people hopped from the vehicles with cameras and rushed towards their car.

"When did this start?" Lora asked her mother.

"They camp out there most of the time. The bus drives down to the house for Melodie now." Janice slowed down, but continued to drive through the aggressive paparazzi. One photographer was so bold that he jumped in front of the car and lay on the hood, snapping pictures. He had a baseball cap on backwards, and his long blond hair hung out from beneath it. He rolled off and shouted, "Thanks." Janice was beeping her horn in an attempt to drive the intruders aside.

"I don't mind them taking *my* picture, but I wish they would leave my family alone." Lora declared.

"It's not too bad. They mostly keep their distance." Janice pulled into the open garage. David's truck was already there. "Oh good, a family dinner tonight." She turned off the ignition and pushed the button to close the garage door. Once the door was closed, they exited the car. "We do it this way because they have telephoto lenses. Your father had the security system expanded, also. I'll give you the codes." After they were all inside, Janice turned and punched some numbers into the box next to the interior, garage door.

Lora set the take-out bags on the counter, in the kitchen, just as her father walked in. "Hi Honey, good to have you home."

"Yes, I come bearing gifts." Lora teased, and gave him a loving hug.

"I hope that's dinner. I'm starving."

Lora gave Melodie a stack of plates, "Will you put these on the table, sweetie? Poppa will bring the drinks out.-And then go wash up for dinner."

"OK, Mimi. Melodie said. "I'm hungry too!"

Lora washed her hands in the kitchen sink and began removing the cartons from the bags. She inserted spoons, and took them to the center of the table. Melodie was already back and seated next to poppa with her impatient legs swinging. "Poppa, would you please help Melodie fix a plate before she falls out of that chair from hunger." She winked at her dad.

"We wouldn't want anything like that to happen," he teased.

While they were eating, Lora's cell phone rang three times. Twice it was her agent and once was the lawyer. She turned off the phone until they were done eating. Family time was just that, time for family, not work interruptions. She had learned that from her father. He never took a call during family dinner time. Even her mother would turn off her phone during dinner and return calls later, if someone left a message.

After dinner, Janice cleaned up, while Lora took her daughter upstairs to bath her and brush out her long, soft, dark hair. Then they read a story, together. Melodie was just beginning to learn to read and would shout out a word that she recognized. Lora was very impressed and told her how proud she was of her. When Melodie was tucked soundly into bed, Lora went to her room to phone her agent. After a short conversation, she showered, got dressed for bed, and joined her parents in the den. It was a chilly fall night, and David had a fire in the fireplace.

"Come and tell us all about New York, Honey." Janice was sitting in a green, wingback chair on one side of the fireplace, her father was in a brown, recliner on the other side, and Lora went to the love seat directly in front of the fire.

"It was all so exciting! I went shopping on Fifth Avenue. I got an outfit at Sak's and some things at H&M's. I have to take Melodie to FAO Schwarz. It was so much fun. I got her some paper airplanes we can build together. I had a private car and driver, at my disposal, the whole time. They really spoiled me. The cameras were a bit much. It was a little unnerving having people shout out your name from all directions."

"I watched you on TV with Mel. You looked wonderful. I was so proud of you," Janice beamed.

"How was the press and paparazzi? They didn't hound you too much, did they?" David asked.

"It wasn't too bad. Molly was with me all the time, and she knows how to handle them."

"So what's next?" her dad asked.

"I just spoke to Molly and she has a studio booked for next month. She wants to get the CD on the shelves for Christmas. She's setting up a photo shoot for the cover, and we're going to pick out some songs. I told her I'd like to stay close to home for the photos. We'll go to the Grand Canyon for the shoot and see how they turn out."

"That sounds good. The closer to home, the better I like it," David said.

"Dad, I'm an adult now. You have to let me spread my wings a little, sometimes," Lora teased.

"We know," her mother said. "We don't mean to smother you."

"I don't feel smothered," she lied. "I know you only want the best for me and want me to be safe and happy. I feel the same way about Melodie." Lora got quiet and looked at her mother, "I don't know what I'd do if something ever happened to her. It scares me to think what I might be capable of."

"We'll protect her, for you, when you're away. Rest assure, she *will* be safe." David said.

"I am glad to see you beefed up security at the house. No sense taking any chances," Lora told her father. Lora's cell phone rang. She answered it, "Hello?" [No answer]. "Hello?" [Still no answer]. She hung up. "Must have been a wrong number." Lora shrugged and put the phone in the pocket of her robe. "If you two don't mind, I think I'll turn in. I'm exhausted from the trip."

"Yes, that's a good idea. Mel needs to be ready for school by eight in the morning." Janice told Lora.

"Why don't you sleep in, mom, I'll get up with Mel and get her ready for school."

"Thank you that might be nice."

"I know things are somewhat chaotic, now, thanks to me. I want to help in any way I can, to lessen the impact. I'm sorry for the cameras outside. I'll see if anything can be done about that. Good night." Lora left the room.

"She appears to be handling things well. Don't you think?" Janice asked her husband.

"She appears to be, so far. She looked a little pale and drawn to me."

"Yes, this is a faster pace than she is used to. I hope she has a few days to regroup." Janice was standing now. "I think I'll turn in too."

David stood, "He kissed his wife. I'll just make sure the alarms are all set and be right in."

The next morning Lora was up early, fixing pancakes and sausage for breakfast. She packed a lunch for Melodie and had the pink princess lunch-box setting on the counter ready to go. Melodie was sitting at the table dressed in her blue, plaid jumper uniform, with a white shirt, navy socks, and black, patent leather shoes. Lora had put her hair in two pony tails with navy ribbons. Lora was amazed at how much her daughter had grown over the summer. *She is a stunning beauty,* Lora thought.

"Mimi, can we build the airplanes when I get home from school?" Melodie asked while chewing.

"May we?" Lora corrected. "Please don't talk with food in your mouth."

Melodie swallowed. "That's what I'm asking." Melodie drank some juice to wash down the pancakes.

"The correct question is -- may we build the airplane after school? – And yes, we may. I want to take you to that store, next time I go. You'll never want to leave. It was fun for me, and I'm all grown up."

Melodie laughed, "But everybody likes to play, even old people, like momma and poppa."

The comment sent chills down Lora's spine. These were innocent words from a child, yet they were a haunting reminder of the past. "Don't fault the child for the sins of the father." Something her priest had said, years ago. Lora had been very careful not to. If only she didn't have those eyes. Melodie was still the most precious thing in her life. Lora sat across from Melodie, sipping her coffee and watching the innocent little girl devour yet another pancake. Just then, David walked into the kitchen.

"Did that little pancake monster leave anything for me?" he teased, kissing Melodie on the head.

"Sure dad, sit down and I'll fix you a plate." Lora went to the cupboard and got a plate for her father. David poured a cup of coffee and sat next to Melodie. Lora set a plateful of pancakes and two sausages in front of her father. She set a knife and fork down along side.

"Wow! This looks delicious. Probably not good for the waistline, though," he joked. David was still as fit as he was in his thirties.

"It was, and I'm stuffed," Melodie said, leaning back in her chair while holding her hands to her stomach.

There came a beep, beep from the school bus. "Let's clean your face. You'd better hurry." Lora wiped Melodie's mouth with a damp cloth and handed her the lunch-box. "I'll be here after school, and we'll work on those planes. Have a nice day, sweetheart. I love you."

"Have a nice day, honey," David called, as Melodie and Lora rushed to the front door. Lora punched in the code and opened the door. Lora smiled as Melodie struggled to climb the big steps of the bus, while carrying the lunch box in her left hand, and gripping the hand bar with the right. Once up the steps, Melodie turned to face her mother, waved, and smiled back.

Lora returned to the kitchen, "Isn't she the most darling thing you have ever seen?" she asked, pouring a second cup of coffee for herself. She went to sit at the table with her father.

"Next to you, that is." David smiled at Lora.

Lora's cell phone, in her robe pocket, began to ring. It was Molly. The photo shoot was a go for Thursday. She should plan on all day at the Grand Canyon, with wardrobe changes and different lighting at different times of the day. Molly told Lora the band needed to have a list of the songs she wanted for the CD. "Great, Molly, I'll have a few days with my family, then. Listen, some camera bugs are camped outside my house. Is there anything that can be done about that?"

"I'm afraid as long as they aren't trespassing; they have a right to be there. I'll alert the police. Maybe they can drive by, to make sure they aren't a nuisance to others on the road. Maybe hassle them a little." Molly offered.

"Thanks, Molly, for everything." Lora turned toward her father. "Well looks like I have a few days to relax. The photo shoot isn't until Thursday."

David noticed a relief wash over Lora. "You are happy, aren't you? I mean, you aren't sorry you did this?"

"Yeah, Dad, I'm happy. It's just, everything seems to be happening so quickly. But, at the same time, it's very exciting."

David kissed Lora on the head. "I'm happy for you then. I'll see you at dinner."

"Yeah. Later dad." Lora went to her room to dress for the day. Her father left for work. She logged onto the computer to check for music she would use on her CD. Her cell phone rang. It was Molly again.

"Your publicist has set up a web page for you. Your fans will be able to check on your appearances and release dates for future albums. He'll also post some of the photos we'll take on Thursday. Check it out. Google your name."

"Cool, thanks Molly. I'll go there now. I'm on the computer." Lora Googled her name, uploaded some photos taken from Celebrity USA, the night she won. There were a few of her performances and a list of the TV shows she had just done. It said she was working on a CD to be released in December. There were a couple of photos of her that were taken on her shopping trip in NY. That made her somewhat uncomfortable; especially a shot of her entering Emma's apartment. There was a caption inferring she and Emma may be more than friends. Lora reached for phone to call her publicist.

"Hey, Paul, I was just looking at this web page. How did a picture of my friend and I get on there with such a suggestive caption? I want that removed." Lora was angry.

"It was sent from an unidentified source. I thought it was titillating and would generated interest.

"But it isn't true! That isn't the kind of interest I'm looking for."

"That doesn't really matter. It will peak peoples interest; Get you noticed. You know what I mean." then Paul added a quip, "No such thing as bad publicity!"

"I can't believe my lawyer let this go. I'm going to give him a call, right now. Please take the picture down immediately," Lora said firmly.

Lora didn't hear her mother at the bedroom door. "You sound upset. Anything wrong?"

"Look at this mom. Some nut case took a picture of Emma and

me, and sent it to Paul, who posted it on my new web page."

Janice looked over Lora's shoulder, at the photo. "That's terrible, Honey. You should warn Emma."

"I will, as soon as I call the lawyer. I hate to think he knew about this, and approved it."

Lora began dialing. Her lawyer seemed genuinely upset and said he would call Paul and deal with him directly. He assured Lora that he had never seen the photo, when he approved the web page layout. "Heads would roll", was the term he used. Lora felt a bit better. After talking to her lawyer, she called Emma and told her about the photo but assured her that she had taken care of the situation. When she went back to the web page , the questionable photo had been removed.

Relieved, Lora went back to picking out songs for the CD. She sought her mother's opinion on the list she had compiled and made some adjustments. She couldn't wait to begin recording. Before she realized it, Melodie's bus had beeped, signaling that it had let her out and was pulling away. When Lora opened the door to greet her daughter, she saw a camera across the street with a long lens on a tripod. She quickly turned her back, got behind her daughter, to shield her from the camera, and hurried her inside the house. She was beginning to realize her life had changed, again, but she was hoping for the better. Seeing the cameras, the photographer's, and the press invading her privacy and that of her family, she was beginning to question that fact.

Chapter Six
A Rising Star
January 2006

ora's CD was released, as planned, in December and flew to the top of the chart, partly through Christmas sales. Her hit single "Forever", which she wrote, was number one for ten weeks. The song was played often on all the radio stations. Melodie grew very excited when she heard it. She knew the words to every song, of course, and sang along. She had a beautiful voice, like her mother. Lora was busy promoting her CD and was required to make numerous appearances across the country. She was spending less and less time at home. Lora still made it a point to phone Melodie every day, because that is what kept her grounded, and was most important in her life.

Lora's picture had been on the cover of all the major magazines. There were, of course, the candid shots in the tabloids, too. Lora grew to expect the negative along with the positive press. She was still uncomfortable with the candid shots that appeared in papers and on the Internet. She had learned that she had no control over what others did, so she concentrated on her music. She wrote some new songs for the CD she planned to record in the spring.

While Lora was at home working on a song on her computer, she took a little break to check out her web page. When she typed in her name a lot of sites came up, as usually did. She went to one and just stared. She was in shock. Lora's nightmare flashed before her, just as if it was happening again right then. She screamed. Janice heard the scream and rushed to Lora's room. She didn't bother to knock, she threw open the door and saw Lora shaking, in her desk chair, in front of her computer. When Janice stood behind her, she saw the image on the monitor. It had been taken at the scene of the rape, nine years earlier. They didn't know that any pictures even existed. The timing couldn't have been worse. It was one month until Melodie's eighth birthday.

Janice wrapped her arms around the visibly shaken Lora. "It will be OK. We'll find out who is behind this. I'll be right back." Janice went to get a phone and called Olivia, the detective that had handled the investigation into the attack. When she got Detective Olivia Marks on the phone, she asked her to have a look at the site. "This picture was taken at the assault scene. The rapist has to be involved in this posting. Maybe this is the lead we have been waiting for." Olivia thanked her and told her to sit tight and she would look into it. Janice pushed the off button on the monitor, and the screen went dark. "Come, let's have a cup of tea, Honey." Janice helped the still shaken Lora from the chair and walked her to the door.

"Mom, it was him. I know it. He knows where I am. What am I going to do?" Lora let herself be led to the kitchen. She sat, heavily, in the wooden kitchen chair, put her elbows on the pine table, and supported her forehead with her hands. She began to weep, softly.

Janice put a teakettle on the stove, to boil, and took two cups from the cupboard. She placed some loose tea in two tiny strainers and set them into the waiting cups. Then she went to the wall phone to call David to let him know what had happened. She needed his support . Janice was trying to be brave, for Lora's sake. But she had, also, been shaken by this latest turn of events. What kind of sick person was this? What else was he capable of? Janice feared for her family.

"Hi, David. There's been a development in the case." Janice waited for David to respond.

"What do you mean a development?" He asked, hearing the strain in her voice.

"A photo, taken at the assault scene has appeared on the Internet."

"Oh my God! Did Lora see it?"

"Yes. I heard her scream and saw the picture on her monitor. She's shaken up pretty badly."

"I'll be right there. We need to notify the Albany police."

"I all ready called Detective Marks. She is looking into it, now."

"I'll be right home." David hung up and rushed to his truck.

"Daddy's coming home. He'll be here soon." Janice poured the steaming water into the cups and carried them to the table. Her hands were trembling. She carefully placed one in front of Lora ; then sat across from her with the other. "It's Chamomile. Be careful, it's hot."

Lora put her hands around the cup and inhaled the steam and aroma to clear her head. She looked at her mother's pained face. "I want to go get Melodie. I want her home with me, so that I know she's safe." Lora sounded terrified.

Janice's heart broke for her. "She'll be safer on the bus. You know how you draw attention every time you go out." She could empathize with her need to protect her daughter. Hadn't she felt the same way about Lora many times before.

"Maybe you're right," Lora said softly, sipping her steaming tea. "Do you think he's out there, in the street right now?" Lora looked wide-eyed at her mother.

Janice reached for Lora's hands and covered them with hers. She felt them trembling. "We're safe in here, even if he's out there."

Lora looked up at her mother, "I should call Molly and Paul, let them know about this. I want them to tighten security." Lora picked up the wall phone. While she was relaying the incident of the photos to Molly, without giving her the specifics of the circumstances surrounding them, her father walked in. Molly was unaware of the assault and Lora wanted to keep it that way. Still, her parents and Emma's family were the only ones who knew; except for the rapist. Looking at her father's grim face, as he was standing by the door, she said, " I have to go. I'll talk to you soon." Lora hung up the phone.

David wrapped his strong, protective arms around Lora, and she broke down and cried hard for the first time since seeing the picture. "I'm so sorry this has happened, Baby." David kissed Lora and continued to hold her, trembling body. His heart broke all over again. "When is this going to be over?" he said, angrily, to no one in particular.

"Not until that creep is caught and punished." Janice said. David looked at her. Janice saw the tears glistening in his eyes.

The phone rang. "Hello?" Janice answered. It was Detective Olivia letting them know they couldn't trace who posted the photo. The site was tracked back to a library in the New York City area. She assured them that she would keep looking into it and call them back. "Thank You Olivia." Janice hung up and relayed the message to David and Lora, who was still in her father's arms. Lora's shoulders sank, but she wasn't surprised. It seemed like this guy was untraceable and untouchable.

"I think it's time we hire a personal body guard for Lora." David was looking over Lora's head to Janice, who was standing with her arms crossed in front of her, to keep her hands steady.

"I think that's a great idea!" Janice nodded her head.

"What do you think about that Lora?" David held Lora back a bit to look into her face.

"Is that what my life has come to? Locked up in my home, surrounded by guards? You would think I am the criminal, here."

"Your mother and I just want you to feel safe, sweetheart, both you and Melodie."

"Yes, of course, I need to think about Mel too."

"OK, I am going to call my lawyer and get a list of names. We'll set up meetings right away." David kissed Lora on the forehead and went to the den to make the call. He touched Janice lovingly on the arm as he walked from the kitchen.

"Mom, this is hell. How can I do this, again? I thought this was behind me. Finally, my life was starting to feel right. I was starting to feel good about myself and comfortable with whom I was becoming." Lora was taking the top off of a bottle of Excedrin. Janice was watching Lora, got a glass of water, and handed it to her. "Thanks mom." She took two pills and sat back down at the table. She laid her now, aching head on her folded arms, on the table.

Janice walked up behind her and massaged the back of her neck. "We'll get through this. There will be an end to this nightmare, one way or another. I promise, darling."

David entered the kitchen. "I got the name of an agency. They're sending over some guys to interview, this afternoon."

"I'm going to lie down for awhile. Do you mind?" Lora was messaging her temple with two fingers.

"Not at all, you go ahead. I'll watch for Mel," her mother offered.

"Thanks, mom, dad, I just have to get rid of this headache." Lora stopped and turned towards her mother. "I should call Emma." She added as almost an afterthought. "I'll do it from my room." Lora walked slowly to her room and closed the door. She sat on her bed and gingerly laid her head back on her pillow, before dialing her best friends number. When Emma answered, Lora told her the grim story of the Internet photos. Emma was in shock, at first. She couldn't speak. The girls cried together and tried to comfort one another. When they ended their brief call, Lora closed her eyes.

"I think a bodyguard is a very good idea, David. I know I'll be less stressed when Lora has to be away for business." David was holding his wife.

"That was my main concern. I'm worried about her going off to New York to record that CD."

Just then, the bus honked its horn. "Oh my gosh! The bus is here." Janice rushed to the front door. She looked up at the vehicles on the main road. They looked so far away, but she knew how close they could get. Janice hugged Melodie and whisked her inside, before the bus pulled away. "Let's go get a snack, Mel and you can tell me all about school, today. Poppa is home early. I'm sure he needs a snack too." Janice took Melodie's back-pack off and set it down by the door, while the eight year old ran to the kitchen calling "Poppa?" Melodie hopped into David's waiting arms and gave him a big hug.

"Momma says you're going to have a snack with me."

"MMM, that sounds like a fabulous idea." David smiled at the little girl, as he set her in the chair, at the table.

"Momma always has great ideas." Melodie's legs were swing-ing back and forth, alternately, under the table and her arms were crossed and laying on the table that came to her upper chest. "Where is Mimi?"

"She had a headache and is lying down." Janice had poured a glass of milk and was spreading peanut butter on some slices of apple. She carried the plate and glass to the table. She set the milk in front of Melodie and the plate within reach of David and Mel. "Dig in."

Melodie, hungrily, reached for a slice and began chewing the crunchy apple slice. David took one for himself. "MMM, I was starving."

"Melodie reached for another, "Me too!"

"Don't they feed you at that school?" he teased.

Melodie giggled, "Of course they do. That was forever ago, though."

"David smiled. The door bell rang and David said, "That was fast. I'll get that." He wiped his mouth on a napkin. "Save some for me, Munchkin." he gave her a quick kiss on the head and (then) went to open the door to what he hoped was the first of the body guard interviews. He was correct. He opened the door. There stood a hulking, six foot three inch, obvious, body builder. He had a dark Mediterranean skin tone and dark wavy hair. He looked at David with dark brown eyes that made it impossible to distinguish his pupil from the iris. His hand shake was definably firm, and he in-troduced himself as Pietro Matzel. *Ah, Italian,* David thought to himself. He was right again. Pietro was born in Italy, but grew up in New York City. He had no accent. Pietro handed David his resume as he led him to his den. They spoke for about half an hour, and

David told him he would be in touch. David had other interviews to conduct before making a final decision. Pete, as he liked to be called, thanked David for his time. Davis walked the giant to the door.

The next candidate arrived an hour later. He wasn't as tall as Pete, only six foot, but still as muscular on his solid black frame. He introduced himself as Rodney Blackman. He was a bit more mature than Pietro, at thirty-four years old, which to David was an asset, as he had more years of experience. Rodney, or Rod, as he preferred to be called, was born and raised in New York City, also; another plus since Lora spent so much time there. David had a comfortable feeling about him,right away. Rod was serious, but showed a good sense of humor. He had even worked on a detail to, then, Governor Pataki. He had a pilot's license and owned a small plane. Rod was an ex marine and had earned a purple heart in the Gulf war, in 1990. His resume was quite impressive.

"If you would wait here, I'd like you to meet my family," David instructed.

"Yes sir," Rod said, as he stood.

"You make yourself comfortable." David went to find Lora, Janice, and Melodie. It wasn't difficult. They were all in the kitchen, helping Melodie with her homework and preparing dinner.

"There is someone I would like you all to meet. He's waiting in the den."

"OK/" Janice wiped her hands on a towel she picked up from the counter.

Lora looked at her father, and he winked at her. "Come along girls, let's not keep him waiting."

Lora stood and pulled Melodie's chair back some to allow her to stand too. They all followed David to the den. "Ladies, I'd like you to meet Mr. Rodney Blackman. He likes to be called, Rod. Rod, this is my wife Janice and my girls Melodie and you're probably familiar with Lora." Rod had stood up when the family entered the room.

Lora stepped forward and extended a hand to Rod, "It's nice to meet you, Mr. Blackman."

Rod shook Lora's hand and said, "Nice to meet you." He tipped his head in Janice's direction and said, "ma'am. Mr. Logan you have a beautiful family."

"Yes I do. Thank you." He smiled at the women. "Janice, if you could finish helping Mel with her school work, I would like Lora to stay and chat for a few minutes."

"Come on, Mel, you can help Momma with dinner." Janice and Melodie holding hands, walked to the open door. Janice turned, "It was very nice to meet you, Rod." Then she continued to the kitchen with Melodie, who could be heard saying, "Who is that?"

David closed the door, gently, and turned to Rod. "Please sit." He gestured to the chair Rod had been sitting in when they entered the room. "Lora, please sit." Lora sat in the second wingback chair, as David went behind the desk and picked up Rod's resume. "Rod has a very impressive resume, here, Honey. Would you like to take a look?" David held out the folder towards his daughter.

"Yes, Thank you." She took the folder and opened it. Her eyebrows raised, she looked up at Rodney. "Yes very impressive, Mr. Blackman."

"Thank you Ma'am."

"If you agree, Lora, I'd like to hire Rod, here, as your bodyguard." David looked to Lora for her reaction to the suggestion.

"Dad, his resume is great. I don't know anything about this, so I'll respect your judgment." Lora handed the folder back to her father, and stood to leave.

Rod stood when Lora did. "I'd just like to say, Miss Logan, I love your music, and it would be an honor to work for you."

Lora looked at him intensely for a moment. He seemed genuinely sincere. He wasn't just feeding her a line in order to procure a job. "Thank-you Mr. Blackman."

"Please call me Rod. Mr. Blackman is my father." Rod smiled at her.

"OK, Rod. I'll let my father work out the details with you. I should go help my mother with dinner; if you both will excuse me."

"That's fine, sweetheart, I'll be there in a few minutes." Lora left and closed the door behind her. She stood there a moment. She couldn't believe this was going to be a part of her life, now. She knew, of course, this sort of thing goes on in the world of entertainment. She just had never thought she would have come this far, this fast. Slowly she walked to the kitchen.

David gave a thumbnail sketch of Lora's needs. He told Rod that risqué photos had been posted of Lora, on the Internet, and he felt that the 'nuts' would be coming out of the woodwork, now. He mentioned that someone seemed to be out to harm her, someone from her past. He didn't volunteer too much more information, other than that. Rod's job would be to make sure no one got too close; plain and simple. He didn't want Lora harmed again. David gave him the name of his lawyer, and Rod agreed to stop by the next day to sign a contract. Then he was to come to the house and meet with Lora to get a copy of her appointments. He would be her "driver", from now on. David, also, called the BMW dealership to arranged–for a white, X3 xDrive 30i, with a lease agreement, to be delivered to the house the next day. He one more call to his lawyer to ask him to draw up a contract for the bodyguard. Now he had to go tell his family the plans he had made. That could wait until after dinner. He went to join them in the kitchen.

Melodie had set the table, as was her job, and Lora and Janice were just putting the serving dishes on. "Perfect timing dear," Janice said, when David walked into the room.

"MMM, smells good, and I'm starving. Someone ate all of my snacks up." He said, looking at Melodie and giving her a wink. Everyone had a seat. Melodie had a hundred questions about the stranger she had met. David explained that Lora needed someone to drive her around, because she had so much to do and so many places to go. "So Mr. Rod will be traveling with Mimi and helping her out," he concluded. Melodie seemed satisfied with the explanation.

"You're so lucky Mimi. Your life is so exciting."

The questions ceased and the family ate in silence until Lora's cell phone rang. She looked at the face and saw the word – unknown. It rang, again. Her father took the phone and answered it, "Hello?" The line went dead. "We'll get you a new phone, tomorrow." He threw the phone into the garbage.

"Poppa, that was Mimi's phone!"

"It was broken. I couldn't hear anybody."

"Maybe it just needs to be charged up. That was wasteful. We learned in school about being wasteful and recycling."

"You know, you're absolutely right. We will recycle the phone." David went to the trash bin where he had tossed the phone, picked it out, gingerly, and wrapped it in a paper towel. He then washed his hands. He would dispose of the phone later. On second thought, he didn't want it in the household garbage, where anyone could get their hands on it, anyway. "Thank you for reminding me, Mel. You are quite the environmentalist, young lady."

"I am?"

"It's good to see that you're learning how to take care of the planet," Lora said.

"Yes, too many adults don't stop to think about that," Janice added.

The family continued with a pleasant dinner, after which Janice and Melodie cleaned up the kitchen, while Lora and David went to the den to discuss how to handle her future as a celebrity.

Chapter 7
The Entertainer
January 2007

Lora had to adjust to having a constant companion that was not a family member. Rod tried his best to make her comfortable when they were alone, yet in public he was all business. Rod called her Miss Lora and was always polite and courteous to all of her business associates. He always had his eyes, behind his dark glasses, watching out for odd behaviors, or actions in Lora's vicinity. He was positioned in the wings at performances and stood guard outside her dressing-room. He was quick to whisk her to exits and safely in and out of wherever she may be staying.

Lora grew very fond of Rod over the last year and was beginning to feel less tense and anxious. She was beginning to write her music again, and her songs were climbing up in the charts. She wasn't able to spend as much time at home as she liked, so Rod became like family to her, while on the road. He told her about his family. He had a sister, Rebeca, who lived in New York City with two nephews, ages 2 and 5, that he adored. He never married, because his job really didn't allow much time for personal relationships. Lora appreciated that. She didn't have much time for a personal relationship, either. She didn't really want one. She didn't care to date. She found it difficult to be alone with a man. She still had trust issues along with other issues, like intimacy. So she just kept busy writing songs and singing, to fill the void in her life.

On a weekend in New York, Lora was in a meeting with her agent and publicist. She told Rod that he should take the afternoon off and visit his family for a few hours. Molly and Paul convinced Rod that Lora would be in the meeting, for several hours, and would be fine. They planned to order out for lunch. Rod agreed, and said he would return by 4PM, and to call if she needed anything. Lora agreed.

"Enjoy your afternoon, Rod." Lora smiled as he headed for the door.

He turned and answered, "Maybe I'll take my nephews to the Bronx zoo. Call if anything comes up."

"Sounds like fun. Wish that I could go. See you later." Lora, Molly, and Paul sat in Molly's office discussing a new album and where to book appearances. Lora insisted on being close to home for the holidays. They planned for an album release, for May, and a summer tour to follow. Lora loved the idea, because Melodie would be out of school and be able to travel with her. They would also try and get a couple of shows in Europe. Melodie would love that. Lora had performed in England, last year, but Melodie was in school, and Lora didn't want to disrupt that. Also, she wasn't as comfortable with her new body guard, at the time. They would need some new photos for the album cover and planned to have them taken next week, while Lora was still in NY. Then she would have a couple of weeks off, before she would return to NY to record. That would fit perfectly with Melodie's winter school break. Maybe she would take her to Disney World, in Florida, for an early birthday present. She couldn't wait to call Mel, tonight, and tell her. Lora's cell phone rang, then. Without hesitation, she answered, "Hello?" [No one responded.] "Hello?" She repeated a little louder. Molly and Paul were laughing over something Molly had said. Then the voice said, "So the little duck is a swan." Lora's hands were visibly shaking. All the color had drained from her face. She still had the phone to her ear, but didn't speak.

Molly noticed her pallor and asked, "Are you OK Lora?" Lora couldn't speak. She was paralyzed with fear.

Paul reached over and took the phone from Lora. "Hello? Who is this?" the phone went dead.

"Who was that Lora?" Paul asked.

Tears were slipping out of the corner of Lora's eyes, no matter how much she tried to blink them back. She wiped them away with the side of her right index finger.

After a couple of minutes, Molly asked, "Lora, what's going on?"

"It's just someone from my past I've been trying to avoid. Now he has this phone number." She tried to sound brave but she wasn't fooling her friends, who had known her for a couple of years.

Molly took the phone from Paul. She tried to see the last phone number that was received "It just said 'unknown'."

Just then there was a light rap on the door, Rod opened it, and poked his head inside. "Miss Lora, I just wanted to let you know that I was back and..." He felt the tension in the room and noticed the still, pale Lora, trembling. "What's going on here?" he asked.

"Lora just got a distressing phone call," Paul answered.

Rod took only four long strides to get to Lora's side. "Is that her phone? Let me have that." He held out his hand toward Molly.

She handed the phone to Rod. "I'll take care of this. I'll be right back." Rod left the room and made a call to a friend at the police department. They had ways of finding out what number was the last one to be received. He messengered the phone to them and asked his friend, Jason, to get back to him, as soon as possible. He returned to the room and said, "Miss Lora is done for the day." He gently took hold of her arm, guided her from the chair and out of the room. Lora didn't resist. She went willingly with Rod to the waiting car in the garage. Rod tried to get her to talk to him, but she remained silent. He had never seen her this way. Rod drove her to her hotel, in silence, and walked her to her room. Once inside Lora's room, Rod asked, "Is there anything you need Miss Lora?"

Lora spoke in a soft voice, "No. Thank you Rod. I just want to call my family."

"I'll be right here if you need anything." Rod went to his adjoining room.

"Thank you Rod. I'll be fine." She said, not very convincingly.

A couple of hours later Rod's cell phone rang. Jason had discovered the phone was a disposable phone and had probably been discarded by now. Rod called David Logan to let him know of the incident and what he had learned of the phone. He assured David that he was on top of things. David relayed the information to Detective Olivia Marks, who was still working on the case from Albany.

Later that night, Rod was lying on his bed when he heard a loud crash come from Lora's room. He knocked on the adjoining door, "Miss Lora?" When she didn't answer, he opened the door, quickly, with his gun raised. Lora was sitting at the desk where seconds ago set her laptop had been, which was now lying on the floor, along with the desk lamp. Rod picked it up and saw an image still on the monitor. It was of Lora, obviously taken this afternoon when she answered the phone. Lora was pale and her eyes were wide with surprise and shock. The bastard had been watching for her reaction and captured it on film. Then he posted it on the Internet. *What was this guy's problem?*, he thought.

"Miss Lora, what did he say to you this afternoon?" Lora had her head on her folded arms at the desk. Rod laid his big hand, protectively, on her shoulder. He could feel her shaking. " Tell me what he said today. Please. Maybe I can help."

Lora lifted her head and stared straight ahead. The curtain was drawn so she wasn't looking at anything. "His exact words were, 'So the little duck is a swan.' That was it."

"What did he mean by that? Do you know? Do you know who it is, or what he wants?"

Lora hesitated before answering. "I don't know his name, but he's someone from my past. Someone who's stalking me, now."

"I think there's something you and your family haven't told me. It might help me to protect you, if I knew everything." He turned Lora's chair to face him. He brought his hulking body down to sit on the edge of her bed so as not to appear so intimidating to Lora.

"My father told me, tonight that it might be time to share everything with you."

"Everything?" He looked puzzled. "So there is more."

"About my past."

"OK. I'm listening." He handed Lora the square box of tissues from the night stand next to the bed.

"Thanks Rod." She took out a tissue and set the box on the now, cleared desk. She wiped her eyes. "This is difficult to talk about. No one but a handful of people know. Not even my agent or anyone in the business."

"I'm very discreet, and it may help if I know everything."

"Yes, I know you are. You've been wonderful Rod." Rodney sat patiently while Lora gathered the strength to tell him what she had never told anyone, before. She began slowly.

"It was ten years ago. I was fourteen. My friend Emma, you know her." Rod nodded affirmatively. Of course he did. He had escorted Lora to meet Emma many times over the last year he had been protecting her.

Lora continued, " We were ... attacked while we were swimming." That's all she could say about it, but Rodney suspected what she really meant.

"And you think this phone call was from your 'attacker'?"

"The guy who... attacked us, took... pictures. We didn't know that then. So far, one of those pictures was posted on the Internet last year. That's when my father hired you. I was getting calls and no one would answer. I change my phone and number every couple of months. Somehow he got this number, anyway."

"Is this the first time he has spoken?"

"Yes. And then this picture." She pointed at her lap top lying on the floor.

"I assume this guy was never punished."

"No he was never found. Detective Olivia Marks is still on the case. She works in the Albany area, where the 'attack' took place."

"OK, so now I know someone is stalking you. This is very helpful. Can you describe what he looks like for me? So that I can keep my eye out for him?"

"I can tell you what he looked like ten years ago."

"I understand that. But anything distinguishing will help."

"I guess his eyes were the most outstanding feature. They are an unusual shade of blue. Very light and ice like."

Rodney registered a look of shock on his face.

Lora saw it. "Yes like my... daughter's."

Rodney was speechless for a just a moment. He composed himself quickly. "That is an unusual color blue. I will keep my eyes out for that. Of course he could wear sunglasses to conceal them. I know he likes to take pictures. All this is helpful. I take it he doesn't know about the child?"

"No-one does, but Emma and her family. My parents moved us to Arizona and have raised her as my sister ever since she was born. Of course Mel knows that I'm her mother."

"Let's keep it that way." Rod told her.

"Thank you. I wish they would just get him and lock him up so Emma and I can put this behind us. We've tried so hard to go on with our lives."

"It seems he's getting a little bolder. He'll make a mistake, and we'll get him. I can promise you that." Rod put his hand on Lora's hand that was resting in her lap. "Now, can I do anything for you tonight?"

"I want to take a shower and turn in," she said feebly.

"Keep the drapes drawn. If you need anything, just knock on my door. I'm a light sleeper, as you know by now." He stood to leave, and Lora stood too. She reached way up to give Rod a hug. Rodney stooped over a bit to hug her back. "Try not to worry, Miss Lora. We'll get this jerk."

"I think I actually feel better having told you. I've been quiet for so long. This has been such a burden."

Rodney went to his room thinking how small and helpless Lora looked, tonight. What a heavy burden she has had to carry all these years, for such a young woman. He was determined to get the bastard. He called David Logan. "I just had a very enlightening talk with Miss Lora. I just wanted you to know that the information will be helpful in my job." Rod didn't want to reveal too much over the phone. You never know who might be listening.

David was thankful for Rod's professionalism and his abilities. Still, he couldn't help but wonder what this lunatic had planned next. He hoped he was staying one step ahead of him, but the fact that he kept getting Lora's phone number was disturbing. This guy needed to be stopped! Thankfully, Rodney felt the same way. Rodney had developed a protective fondness for Lora. This made David feel a sense of relief. He hoped Rod would be even more diligent in his efforts to protect his daughter.

Lora tossed and turned all night. She kept hearing voices in her head – his voice, speaking into her ear; vile words, laughing; breathing. She smelled the alcohol on his hot breath. She couldn't breathe. She felt his weight on her. He was smothering her. Lora screamed and sat straight up in bed. Rodney burst through the door with his gun in hand for the second time that night. Rodney looked around the room and saw that everything was secure, thus surmising Lora had a nightmare. "Bad dream?" he questioned. "If you don't mind, Miss Lora, I 'd like to stay in the room with you. I'll just sleep in that chair." He gestured toward the chair next to the dresser. He pulled a blanket and pillow from the top shelf of the closet, never giving Lora the opportunity to object. Rod settled in the chair and spread the blanket over his lap and chest. He laid his head at an angle on the pillow propped at the side of his head. He closed his eyes. Lora just watched him in amazement, sighed, and laid down. Rodney could hear the even breathing soon after and knew she had fallen asleep. He hoped she would sleep through until morning.

Chapter 8
The Stalker
February 2007

Lora picked up a new cell phone every two weeks. So far she hadn't received any more calls. She worked on songs for her new CD and was returning home to her family to take Melodie on a vacation to Walt Disney World, in Florida. She had been working nonstop, writing new music and rehearsing. She was ready for a break, before recording the CD and going on a summer tour. She had Molly book two adjoining executive rooms at the Hilton at Disney World. Rod was going to fly them down in his private plane. Lora was in her hotel room, packing when the room phone rang. She picked it up thinking it was the front desk. "Hello?"

"You can't avoid my calls." It was the stalker.

Lora froze for a moment. "What do you want? Leave me alone!"

"Why would I want to do that? You're so much fun. Did you think I had forgotten?" He laughed. She remembered that laugh. She hated hearing it again. Lora was about to hang up. "Don't worry, we'll be together soon." He hung up.

Gooseflesh rose on her skin. "Rod!" she called.

Instantly, Rod appeared from his door. "Miss Lora?"

Lora still had the receiver in her hand. "He just called on the room phone."

Rod took the receiver from her, hung it up, and pushed the button for the front desk. "Please trace the last call to this room." They waited a moment. "Sir that call came from a pay phone in the lobby," the front desk clerk told Rod.

"Miss Lora, I'm going to have a look in the lobby. Lock the doors and don't open them for anyone." Rod locked her door and slipped the chain on then left through his door. He took the elevator to the lobby and strolled around, looking at everyone. He found the pay phones empty except for a woman in the end one. He looked in the gift shop, and coffee shop, then went to the dining-room, but didn't spot the blue-eyed stalker. He hurried back to his room, and knocked on Lora's door. "Miss Lora?"

Lora opened the door. "Did you see him?"

"Afraid not. What did he say?" Lora relayed the caller's threat. "Hmm, He's really getting bold. He'll make a mistake -- they all do – and when he does, I'll get him," Rod reassure Lora.

"I'll feel better once we leave NY. My bags are all set. Could you have the bell boy take them to the car?"

"Yes, Miss Lora."

And, Rod, could you please stop calling me Miss Lora. Just Lora is fine. You make me feel so old. It must be about the same as me calling you Mr. Blackman."

Rod smiled and nodded, "Certainly, Lora, if you prefer."

"You're like a family to me. You know as much about me as my family. Let's not be so formal."

"I pulled the car up to the exit in the garage. We can follow the bags out, if that's Okay. We can be on the road in less than twenty minutes."

"That sounds perfect," Lora sighed with relief,-"I just want to stop by and see Emma in Albany. I know it's out of the way. I just need to see her." Lora picked up her cell phone. "I'll tell her we'll be there in a few hours."

Rod called the front desk, on the room phone, and asked for assistance with the bags. A young man knocked on the door within five minutes. Rod answered the door, showed the uniformed man the bags, and asked him to get the ones in the adjoining room. He stacked the bags on the gold handled, rolling cart. "We're all set here...mmm, Lora." Rod wasn't use to calling her just Lora.

She winked at Rod and smiled. She held up her pointer finger indicating she would be one minute. She said goodbye to Emma and put her phone in her pocket. Lora grabbed her purse from the desk and followed the gold cart, with her bags, while Rod, close behind her, shut the door.

They rode the elevator to the garage floor, where Rod stepped out first to look around. "This way." He put his arm in Lora's and walked her to the car quickly. Once at the car, he opened the door, and Lora slipped into the passenger's seat. Rod had pushed the trunk release and the baggage boy loaded the bags. Rod slipped the young man a tip and closed the trunk. He hopped into the driver's seat and they were off without incident. They headed out of the city and onto the thruway, toward Emma's. Lora and Emma had planned to meet, halfway, at an out-of-the-way dinner.

Lora and Rod talked about the upcoming vacation to Florida. He was going to check into the security at the hotel. The plane was being gone over. It would be in tip-top condition for the flight next week. Lora decided to call home and let her parents know they would be stopping to see Emma for about an hour. "You know, Rod, Molly is going to get me a tour bus. It's going to be outfitted with a sleeping area for you. You won't have to drive."

"Is that so? Miss...I mean, Lora."

"Can you believe it-- little Lora Logan, – a big star with a tour bus and bodyguard? I never dreamed my life would be like this. I just wanted to make music and bring a little joy to the world. I never dreamed I would be so well received"

"You certainly have a lot of fans. My nephews even listen to your songs. They're big fans, too."

"Well, I'll autograph a CD for them," she offered.

"Oh, they would really love that." Rod smiled at her. "Thank you."

"Why didn't you tell me this before?"

"I didn't want to take advantage of our relationship."

"Are you serious? If there is anything I can ever do for you, or your family, don't hesitate to ask. Please Rod, you're so special to me."

"You're a extraordinary woman, Lora Logan. All this fame and yet you are so down to earth. I have worked for some, let's say, stuck-up clients, before. Fame and money went straight to their heads."

"Ever work for one with a stalker, before?" Lora was curious.

"As a matter of fact, I have, and I got her. It was a woman stalking a married client of mine. She was up front about it, though, not underhanded like yours. Yours has something to lose by being found out. He must know the authorities are after him?"

"I don't know. He may not know we reported it, since he's been free all these years."

"That would be even better. When he comes out of hiding, we'll catch the bastard. Excuse my language."

"Can I tell you something? Promise you'll keep it between us?"

"You can tell me anything, Lora. You should know that."

"I've dreamed of him coming back. I kill him in my dream. Is that horrid of me?"

"I think it's only natural to want to hurt the person who hurt you. You want him to stop being a threat to your friend and family. Hell, I want to kill him for what he's doing."

"Does that make me a bad person?" she asked.

"It makes you human." Rod laid his big dark hand on her thigh of her blue jeans.

Lora set her small hand on top of his. "Thanks for saying that."

"Well, here we are. Let's go in and have a look, make sure Emma is here, and then I'll leave you to your visit." Rod pulled up in front of the dinner. It wasn't crowded, only five cars in the parking lot and a big rig off to the side.

Lora and Rod walked in together. They always got stares when they went anywhere. He was a large black man with a petite white girl. No one seemed to recognize that she was Lora Logan, sometimes. Rod walked her to a booth in the back. Just then Emma walked in and waved. She sat across from Lora, "Hi Rod. It's good to see you. How have you been?"

"Things are good, Miss Emma. Enjoy your visit. I'll be just over there at the counter."

Rod sat at the counter with his back to the girls. He ordered a coffee and slice of chocolate cream pie. The wall across from him was mirrored, which allowed him to have a view of the door and keep an eye on the girls. The only other customer at the counter was the truck driver, who was having his dinner. A young couple was in a booth, having sandwiches, fries, and soda. There was an older couple that starred at him when he entered with Lora. They were still whispering and staring; they were harmless. Rod saw the waitress approach the girls and take their order. She returned a few minutes later with drinks. A single man entered the dinner, and Rod watched him take a booth not far from the girls. He was wearing a black baseball cap, denim jacket, over a black tee shirt, and black cargo pants. He was wearing dark glasses. Rod kept his eye on him. The waitress brought the girls their orders and went to take the stranger's. He was joking, or flirting with her. Rod couldn't hear him. The waitress giggled at whatever he said. The stranger smiled back at her. She brought him a cup of coffee and set some cream on the table. The stranger looked up at Rod in the mirror and smiled as he poured the creamer into his coffee. Rod didn't like this. He had a bad feeling about this stranger. He got up and walked to the guy. Lora saw Rod get up walk to a booth without sitting. She hadn't seen the stranger come in and sit. She didn't like this. She saw him talking to someone but couldn't hear what he was saying. He didn't look happy.

"We might have to leave quickly Emma. Something isn't right with Rod. I don't like his expression."

Rod walked up to the stranger's booth, "Do I know you?" he asked.

"I don't know where we would ever have met." He stirred his coffee, still smiling smugly.

"It's just the way you were smiling. seemed like you knew me."

"Nope, I'm just a friendly, fun loving sort of guy, or so I've been told." he didn't look up at Rod.

Rod walked to Lora's booth. He set some money on the table and told the girls he thought it was time to leave. They didn't argue. They both slipped from their seats. Rod took the girl's arms and walked them to the exit. They heard the stranger laugh as they walked past. The older couple's jaws dropped. Rod walked Emma to her car and then Lora to theirs. He waited until Emma left the parking lot, safely, before leaving, to make sure no one followed her. "Something isn't right with that dude." That's all an explanation he gave as they drove off in the opposite direction.

Back at the dinner, Doug Civics was smiling to himself as he drank his coffee.

Stupid bitches thinks I don't know what they're doing, he thought. He had already taken pictures of them as they entered the diner. He was thinking of all the different spins he could put on them for captions. He was making a bundle off Lora Logan. Good thing she was a stupid little kid who never turned him in all those years ago.

She sure grew up pretty. 'Wouldn't mind a piece of that, now. HMMM, never did get piece of that other one. Might try that. He put a bill on the table and went to his motorcycle that was parked on the other side of the big rig. *That tap on Emma's phone is real handy. I think I'll just pay her a little visit.* He drove off in the direction Emma had taken. He hoped she was going straight home.

He smiled to himself as he rode. His mind planning what he had in store for little Emma. She wasn't as young and stupid as before. He'd been watching her. He'd have to be very crafty. Charm won't work this time. He'd just take what he wanted and get Lora Logan's attention at the same time. What was it about that broad that kept him hooked? He tried, but just couldn't get her out of his mind. Maybe if she was dead he could be rid of her. He needed to get close to her. *Maybe this Emma bitch is the key.*

Doug got more excited at the prospect of getting to Lora through Emma. He had a whole plan thought out, by the time he pulled up in the alley, behind her apartment house.

Chapter 9
Emma's Revenge
February 2007

*L*ora and Rod decided it might be better to change their plans and drove to the nearest airport. They would fly home. Rod chartered a plane, and they got their baggage loaded. Rod made arrangements to have the car driven to Flagstaff. Lora called her parents to let them know that she would be home in the morning. Rod would rent a car at the airport when they landed. David and Janice were alarmed and concerned with the sudden change in plans, but trusted Rod's judgment. He would fill them in when they met.

Rod and Lora were in the air by the time Doug pulled his motorcycle up to the street that ran behind Emma's apartment. He had done this many times before. He knew the shortest route to take, to get his pictures, and get out before being seen. He wanted more than a picture, tonight. He was angry about that goon at the diner.

That goon was always in the way. Well, not tonight.

Doug went to the street and looked up at Emma's window.

Good, the lights were on. She was home. He left his jacket in the saddle bag of the bike and took out his small movie camera. He was dressed in black, making it hard to be seen in the dark alley. Doug went to the back of the house and stealthy crept up the fire escape to the second floor, in the rear of Emma's apartment.

Stay calm, he told himself. *Don't make a sound. Don't blow it now, after all this time.* The window was open a crack. *Thank God for a warm winter in the city.* He put his ear to the crack in the window and listened. He could hear the shower running in the other room. *Sweet, could this bitch make this any easier for me?"* He removed the screen from the window, with a knife he always carried, and slowly raised the window. He was so proud of himself and with the quiet, efficient way he moved. Years of practice. He slipped his trim body through the open window and tiptoed towards the sound of the running water. The door was open, alloying steam to pour into the hallway. It would be so easy to grab her in the shower. *No, wait until she is in bed,* he thought. Doug went to the bedroom and found a hiding place in the louvered-doored closet. Emma had her nightie laid out on the down-turned bed. The radio next to the bed was on. *How nice,* he mused, *a Lora Logan song.* He could hear Emma singing to it in the shower. *You suck. You are no Lora Logan,* he thought.

I haven't forgotten how playful you were back then little Emma. Maybe you are even better now. The water went quiet. *Get all nice and sweet smelling for Smilin' Jack.* Doug was watching through the louvers. He was almost giddy with excitement.

Emma walked to the bed, naked, and slipped the nightie over her head. She had kept her hair dry, in a towel, and removed it to let her silky hair fall free. She began combing it out. Doug could hardly stand it. Then Emma stood up suddenly. *Why is it so cold in here?* She left the room. Doug couldn't see her, but he heard her close the kitchen window. *Stupid, I should have closed that window again.* He could hear Emma checking the other windows and doors. She returned to the bedroom, set her alarm, and turned off the radio and the light.

Doug waited. When he could hear her breathing evenly he knew she was asleep. There was a little moonlight coming through the window, across the room, and it shone on Emma in her bed. She was sleeping on her stomach, with one hand under her pillow.

This is almost too easy, Doug thought to himself. He pushed open the closet door silently, slowly. He moved like a ghost to the foot of her bed. She never stirred. He pulled a small camera, he always carried, from his cargo pants' pocket. He set it to record and placed it on a dresser, under the window, and went back to the bed. He removed his cargo pants and dropped them on the floor next to the bed. Then he peeled the covers back, slowly, to reveal Emma's sleeping body. He picked up the second pillow from her bed and held it above her head.

Can't have you make any noise, bitch. He brought the pillow down over Emma's face and head as he straddled her body. Emma awoke, instantly, and began to squirm and shout. The sound was muffled but the squirming was just what Doug had hoped for. "Yeah, still playful," he said.

Emma stopped a moment when she heard his voice. She didn't have to see, to know who he was. Emma began fighting back in earnest. Her nightie was up to her neck. Her breast was exposed on one side. Doug was sitting on top of her legs, still holding the pillow over her head.

"Now stop yelling and I'll take the pillow away."

Emma didn't move to indicate she understood. Doug was still

sitting on her and had her pinned down. He started to lift the pillow. Emma stayed quiet.

"That's a good girl." He tossed the pillow to the floor, while holding the back of Emma's neck down to the bed, so she couldn't pick her head up. Any sound she tried to make would still be muffled by the pillow under her face. Her hand was still under the pillow. "Remember how much fun we had?" He was driving her legs apart with his leg. Emma began to squirm again to fight her attacker off of her. He hit her on the back of her head. "So you like it rough, now. That's fine with me." He hit her again, now, and turned her over. "You grew up as nice as your friend Lora Logan."

"Please, don't hurt me," Emma pleaded.

"I'm not going to hurt you. We're just having some fun. You still like to have fun, don't you?'"

Emma tried to knee her attacker in the groin, but missed and got him in the stomach. She heard the air escape his mouth. "Let me go!" she shouted.

"Well, since you asked so nicely." He wheezed out. He hit her hard across the face, splitting her lip and blackening her left eye. "Now, how about some fun, bitch." Doug pulled her leg up over his shoulder so that she couldn't try and knee him again. She had no leverage. She was open to his attack. He was holding her right hand down to the bed.

Emma's left hand was still under her pillow. She was gripping a six inch steak knife. She had taken to sleeping with a knife, ten years ago, much to the chagrin of her parents. Doug was intent on perpetrating his attack. He didn't see Emma's hand, with the knife, come from under the pillow. Out of the corner of his eye, the moon light hit the blade, just before it was about to plunge into his side. He deflected it, but it sliced his arm. "Shit!" He hit Emma hard, again, and twisted her arm, breaking it. The knife fell to the floor. Doug's arm was bleeding, profusely. She must have hit a vein or something. The enraged man hit Emma across the face so hard she lost consciousness. Doug got off the bed and pulled his pants on with one hand. He was already feeling a bit light headed. He grabbed his camera from the dresser, as he hurried from the room, leaving a trail of blood behind.

Somehow, he made it down the front stairs and around back to his bike. He wrapped his shirt tightly around the bleeding arm, threw on his jacket, and rode to a secluded spot under a bridge. He had a friend who was a veterinarian. He would have to get to him and get this taken care of. "I'll be back bitch."

Emma was in extreme pain when she regained conscientious. After a few minutes, she was able to punch in 911 with her right hand. She wrapped her blanket around her body and passed out, again, from the pain. The next thing she remembered was the paramedics taking care of her in her apartment. The police were there as well. She told them what she could before she was taken to the hospital. She told them she wanted to talk to Detective Olivia Marks. They said they would send for her, to talk to Emma at the hospital.

Rod and Lora landed safely in Flagstaff. Rod had called ahead, and a rental car was waiting for them at the airport. Their baggage was loaded into the trunk, while Lora went to the restroom to freshen up. Rod also took the opportunity to freshen up and splash water on his face. It had been a long day, and he wanted to remain sharp. He was through before Lora so he waited for her just outside the woman's room door. "All set?" he asked, when she came out.

"Yes, Let's get home. I could sleep for a week."

"I know how you feel" Rod walked close to her and opened the passenger door to the rented car. When Lora was safely inside, he closed the door and crossed in front to get into the driver's seat. "Should be home in a few minutes, now. I called ahead to let security know we're coming. They'll step up their watch."

"You think of everything. What would I do without you, Rod?"

"Why don't you close your eyes for a few winks?"

"Try and stop me." Lora laid her head back and fell asleep within minutes.

Rod passed security at the, recently installed, gate at the entrance to the Logan ranch. He drove to the rear of the house, where another garage had been built to allow for more privacy from the road.

Lora awoke when Rod turned off the engine. She blinked her eyes. "Home sweet home." She smiled at Rod. "Thank you, for everything." Rod went around the car and opened her door. He held her hand as she climbed out.

David was waiting at the door. "Yes, thank you Rodney. You can turn in. Your room is ready for you. I'll take her from here." David put his arm around Lora and walked her into the kitchen, closing the door behind them.

"Yes Sir, Mr. Logan." David had built an apartment over the garage for Rod. It had knotty pine walls and floors. Blue plaid curtains hung at the windows overlooking the creek. He had a kitchenette, living-room, with a pellet stove, and spacious bedroom, with a king size bed. Rod couldn't wait to hit the shower and go to sleep.

Emma had been taken to surgery, to have pins put in her broken arm. They did a rape test, even though she told them she hadn't been raped. She asked them not to contact any one, yet. She was sleeping peacefully with the pain medication she had been given.

Detective Olivia was sitting in the room when she awoke at 10:00 AM the next morning.

A nurse was taking her temp and vitals for her chart."How are you feeling?" she asked.

"Like I was hit by a car." Then she saw the detective. "Oh, Detective Marks. I'm so glad you're here."

"I've been waiting for you to wake up. How are you doing? Up for some questions?"

"Please, I want this guy caught before he gets to Lora, again."

"You think this was the same man, and that's what he has planned?"

"Yes, it was him, for sure. I got him this time, before he could get me."

"Yes we found a great deal of blood at the scene."

"I cut his arm. I sleep with a knife under my pillow. I have for years. It came in handy tonight."

"We found it on the floor, and sent it to the lab. We weren't sure whose it was. You must have hit a vein. He left a trail of blood to the street behind yours. Then it vanished. He got into some sort of transportation. He'll need to have that wound stitched up. We've alerted all the doctors and hospitals to look for a knife wound. We know he entered through a window off of the fire escape."

"I closed an open window before I went to bed. I thought I had left it open."

"Anything else you can remember."

"No, I was in and out of consciousness, I'm afraid."

"We got a lot of DNA from you and the scene. He didn't rape you Emma."

"I know."

"Is there someone I can call for you?" Olivia asked.

"I want to call Lora, myself, so she'll know that I'm OK. If she hears it from anyone else she won't believe them. She'll freak out. I'd like to call my parents, too."

"Well, if you need anything, call me. I have some leads to check out. He was sloppy. We'll get him."

"I hope so. He's gotten away far too long." Emma said.

"Don't leave town without letting me know how to reach you, in case we have more questions."

The nurse came in with a lunch tray. "When may I leave this place?" Emma asked the nurse.

"The doctor will be in later to talk to you. Do you need anything?"

"No,thank you. On second thought, a phone, if you don't mind."

The nurse picked up the phone from the nightstand and set it next to Emma on the bed. "Here you go, Hun."

The nurse left, and the detective walked to the door. "I'll be in touch."

"Thank you detective."

Emma called her parents, first, in Florida, where they spent the winter months, now that they were retired. They returned home, to New York, for the summers. "Hi Mom." She tried to sound up beat, when her mother answered the phone. She didn't want to alarm them.

"Hi, Emma, How are you?" her unsuspecting mother asked.

"Well, I've had an accident and have broken my arm." She braced herself for her mother's concerned, barrage of questions.

"Oh, honey, what happened? Was it a car accident? Are you alright? Do you need me to come home?"

"No mom, I'll be fine. I may come down there for a couple of weeks while I'm healing, though."

"That's a great idea. We'd love to have you. Please do come, honey."

"I'll call in a day or so. I love you mom."

"We love you too, Hun. Dad says Hi."

Emma had to hang up. She was starting to cry and didn't want her mother to hear that she was frightened. She got it out of her system and was about to call Lora, when her doctor came in. "How are you doing Emma?"

"Why don't you tell me?"

"Okay, your arm was fractured in two places. We needed to put in a pin to hold it while it heals. You will be in the full cast and sling for six weeks. Then, we will cast only the lower half of your arm for another four weeks, after we remove the pins. When the cast comes off, you will need several weeks of rehabilitation. The rest of your injuries are minor and will heal in a few weeks. I'll give you a prescription for pain, of course."

"When may I leave?"

"I'd like you to stay until tomorrow, to make sure you don't develop an infection. If you remain fever free, then I don't see why you can't go home."

"Thank you, doctor" Emma actually felt relieved that she wasn't injured worse, or killed.

"I'll check on you this evening." The doctor left the room, carrying his clipboard, and jotting a note on her chart.

Emma had to call Lora; she had to warn her. She dialed Lora's cell number and waited for Lora to answer. "Hello?"

"Hi, Lora. Where are you now?" She was thinking Lora and Rod were still driving.

"I'm home. After that scene at the diner, Rod chartered a plane, and we flew home,"

"I'm so glad, Lora." She knew she would be safe there.

"Why, what's wrong? Don't lie to me, because I can tell something is wrong. I can hear it in your voice."

Lora and Emma were so close that she had no doubt Lora could tell something was wrong. She just had to tell her, straight out. "Lora, I was attacked last night. Now before you flip out, let me talk." Emma was talking faster, now, to make sure she got everything said.

"Oh my God Emma! How? Where?"

"Listen. It was at my apartment. He broke in and attacked me, but I had my knife under my pillow. I fought back and drove him away, before he could do anything."

"My God! Are you all right?"

"I have a broken arm. I'll be fine."

"I'll fly out, today!"

"NO! Please don't"

"Emma what haven't you told me?"

Softly, Emma told Lora, "Lora, It was ... him. It's not safe, for you, here in New York"

Lora was silent on the other end. "You're sure? It was *him*?"

"Yes, Detective Marks is working on it now. I got him good with my knife, Lora. I sliced his arm open."

"I want you to come and stay at the ranch with me. You'll be safe here."

"I have to stay in the hospital, at least until tomorrow. I have to let the detective know where I'll be."

"I'll send Rod for you. He'll fly you out to stay with us. Melodie and I are going to Florida for a couple of weeks. I want you to go with us. We'll have lots of security. We could visit your parents.

They must be so upset, Emma."

"Actually, I only told them I had an accident and broke my arm. I'll wait until I'm with them to tell them the story. They'll be so worried, otherwise, Lora. They do want me to come to their house."

"You're right. No since upsetting them. I'll make arrangements with Rodney and call you back later. Is there anything I can do for you, in the meantime?"

"You're the best, but I'll just sleep for awhile. Really. I'll be fine."

"Okay, Emma, I'll call later with the details. I love you girl."

"Back 'atcha." Emma hung up and laid the phone on the blanket next to her leg. She fell asleep that way.

Lora told her parents about the attack on Emma. They were extremely upset but, even more so when Lora told them she was flying to Albany to get her friend. It wasn't that they didn't approve of Emma coming to the ranch. They didn't want Lora in New York. Rodney arranged for the charter plane and filed flight plans to and from Albany. He called a buddy, in Albany that he knew from his years protecting the governor. He agreed to sit outside of Emma's room, at the hospital, until he arrived to get her.

Detective Marks called David to tell him about the progress in the case. The DNA they got from the scene at Emma's, matched ten other rape scenes, in the New York area, alone. "This guy has been very busy." She told him. These cases date back two years before Lora's attack."

"How many women in all?" David asked.

"We don't have that information from every state, yet. I should have that tomorrow."

"Listen, Lora is flying into Albany to get Emma, tomorrow. I want to know she will be safe," David stated sternly. He had lost all faith in the police, after this latest attack and subsequent news of multiple rapes.

"Mr. Logan, we'll do everything we can to protect your daughter. We have a plain clothes officer watching Emma's apartment and someone at the hospital watching her room. Emma wounded this guy pretty badly. I think he'll be holed up, somewhere, if he isn't dead."

"I just don't want to take any chances. This guy is nuts! I hate to think what I might do if I get my hands on him." David's hands were shaking with anger.

"We're going to get this serial rapist. He's making too many sloppy mistakes not to be found out. We're putting an artist sketch on the TV news channels."

"It's not like you didn't do that last time. You got nothing then."

"This guy is very clever, or should I say, *was* very clever. I think his fixation on Lora is what will do him in." Detective Marks was trying to calm and reassure David. One thing she didn't need was an irate father getting in the middle of her investigation.

"If anything happens to these girls, I'm holding you and your department personally responsible. This has to end, and soon!" David slammed the phone down. How much more of this were they suppose to take. "Desperate times call for desperate measures." David picked up his cell phone and punched in some numbers. After a few moments, he spoke. "I want to talk. One hour!" He hung up, and poured a sip of vodka to steady his hands.

Two hours later, Lora and Rod were boarding the plane for Albany. They would, again, pick up a rental car at the airport and go straight to the hospital. Lora was anxious to see if Emma was really all right. She knew what this pervert was capable of. She had been having flash backs since she heard his voice on the phone. She hadn't told anyone about it. Everyone was enough on edge as it was. She noticed a change in her father and wondered if it was just last night, or if he been acting agitated for awhile? She was about to ask her mother about it, when Emma called. She made a mental note to talk to her mother, when she returned home.

"You're very quiet, Lora. Anything you want to talk about?" Rod said, looking over at Lora.

"I'm just concerned about Emma. I'll feel better when I see her. She said she got him good, with her knife."

"If he survives that, he'll have a nasty scar to show for it; just another way to identify him."

"Did you hear that he's been doing this sort of thing since before my attack, ten years ago? Detective Olivia called him 'a serial rapist'."

"… And you were wondering what your life would have been like if he had been caught before … well, just before, you know." Rod was feeling a bit awkward talking to Lora about the "attack". He couldn't believe the rage that would fill him whenever he thought about, and realized that pervert was after her again. He just wasn't going to allow that to happen. If the authorities couldn't catch him, he would. Somehow he was going to put a stop to this guy. A sly smile spread across his face. *You think you're so tough picking on women. Wait until we meet,* he was thinking.

"Of course I wonder, what if..? But Rod, I love my daughter and wouldn't change the fact that I have her in my life. I worry about what kind of world she was born into, and will I be able to keep her safe? I see what this has done to my parents. My mother has had to be a mother to her granddaughter. It wasn't supposed to be this way."

"Life throws us curves, and we have to be flexible and bend with them. You have a beautiful family. I could feel the love in that house, the first time I was there. That's the world you brought Melodie into."

"Love isn't enough, sometimes." A tear ran down her cheek. Rodney reached over with his large hand and gently wiped it from her face with his thumb. Lora reached for his hand and held it to the side of her face. "I feel so safe with you." She kissed his hand.

Rodney watched her gentle move. He was touched by her act. "I won't let anything bad happen to you. I promise." He spoke softly. He had a special affection for Lora. An affection that was clearly unprofessional. He tried to fight it, but little moments like these drew him closer to this woman. He dared not show Lora how he felt for fear of frightening her.

Lora was so confused by her feelings. at that moment, she wanted Rodney to put his muscular arms around her and hold her. She wanted to sink into his chest and be comforted by the rhythmic, steady beat of his heart; his big, generous heart. She felt that he thought of her as more than just a client. She hoped so, no; she prayed so. Lora wondered if Rod thought any less of her, now that he knew the truth of her past. Somehow she doubted that. That's not the kind of man she knew him to be. But how could she know for sure?

"We'll be landing soon." Rodney busied himself with landing preparations. He was communicating with the airport. Lora's thoughts were on Emma, now. She couldn't wait to see her dear friend.

Once at the hospital, because they were expecting Lora Logan, she was discreetly escorted to Emma's room. Emma was in her room, dressed, and sitting in a visitor chair, just staring out a window that didn't even have a view. She didn't hear the door open. Lora saw a pathetic Emma sitting all alone. Her heart broke for her. When Emma turned her head in Lora's direction, ,her black-and-blue, puffy face made Lora turn red with rage. "My God, Emma. You're *not* fine." She rushed to Emma's chair, just as Emma was standing, and gave her a hug. "We're going to get you out of here and safe with me."

"I'll bet I'm doing better than that jerk is." She sniffed.

"That well may be, but I'm going to take real good care of you. Can you just leave?"

"My release papers have been signed. I do have to fill a prescription."

"We'll take care of that. Do you want to go home and pack some clothes?" Lora asked.

"That would be great."

"We'll drop your prescription off, before going to your place, and pick it up on the way to the airport."

Emma tried to laugh. "Sounds like a plan, girl. Hello Rod." She smiled at Rod who was standing behind Lora.

A nurse arrived with a wheel chair. "Hospital policy. Hop in." Emma didn't object, she sat down in the chair and was wheeled from the room. Lora followed closely, and Rod was right beside her. They exited the same back way they had used to entered the hospital. Rod's car was still parked just outside the door. Lora hopped into the back, and Rod helped Emma into the passenger seat, before closing her door. They went to the drive-thru window of the drug store, left the pain prescription, and then headed to Emma's apartment. With his trained eye, Rod spotted the surveillance vehicle on the street. He escorted the two women inside. Just to be cautious, he had the girls wait by the closed door while he checked each room of Emma's apartment.

"All clear ladies."

Lora and Emma went straight to the bedroom. Lora went to the closet and took out Emma's suitcase. Emma stood in the doorway fixated on the bed. Lora was so busy trying to get Emma out of the city that she hadn't noticed Emma just standing there.

"So, what are you..." Lora looked up and saw Emma, pale faced, standing in the doorway and followed her line of sight, which ended on the bed: a bloodied mass of sheets and blankets. "Rod!"

Rodney hurried into the room fearing the worst. He saw Emma blocking the doorway.

"Please take Emma into the living-room to sit down. I'll throw some things together for her." Lora went through drawers pulling garments out to pack in the suitcase.

Rodney gently turned the statuesque Emma around and guided her to a chair in her living-room. "We'll be out of here soon, he told her. Emma just nodded. "Can I get you anything? A glass of water?"

"Yes, thank you, Rod."

Rod went to the refrigerator and found a bottle of water. He carried it back to Emma, twisted off the cap, and handed it to her. "Is this okay?"

"This is just fine. Thank you. Have one yourself. I should probably clean out the fridge if I'll be gone for awhile."

"I'll do that. We can carry out the trash when we leave."

"You and Lora are so great to help me like this." Emma took a long drink of the bottled water.

"You're as close as family to Lora. She loves you so much. Any friend of Lora's is all right in my book."

"Thanks again, Rod. You're all right, too. Now that we're alone, please keep a close eye on Lora. I'm afraid that nut case is going to go after her. Don't tell her I said that. It will only frighten her."

Rod nodded and went to the fridge. First he dumped the milk down the drain. There were a few take out containers that he tossed into the trash. A couple of pieces of fresh fruit he looked over and decided to eat the peach and toss the pear.

Lora came from the bedroom, pulling the suitcase that was on wheels. "What are you doing Rod?"

"Just cleaning out the fridge, so it won't stink when Emma comes back. Want me to get that suitcase?"

"I bundled the bedding up. Could you stuff it in a bag? We'll just toss it, as well."

Rod looked under the kitchen sink and found some trash bags. He pulled one out of the box and went down the hall to grab the bedding. When he was down by the floor, gathering it up, something caught his trained eye. The receiver on the bedside phone was not setting right. He picked it up and saw the pieces didn't fit right. He pried the back off and saw a listening device inside. Rod called Detective Marks and told her she should come over there and try to get some prints. Another lead. *Yep, this guy is getting too sloppy.* Rod smiled to himself. He finished stuffing the bedding into the bag and carried it out to the front door. "You ladies sit tight while I get rid of the trash." He grabbed both bags, went down to the street, and around to the back by the trash bins. He saw the trail of blood that the police had followed. *Nasty wound that guy had.* Rod went back to the women and grabbed the suitcase. "After you."

They all returned to the car under the watchful eye of the

surveillance car, across the street. A quick stop at the drugstore and they were headed to the airport. The plane had been refueled and was ready to go. Emma slept through most of the flight to Flagstaff. Their rented car was waiting, and several hours after leaving NY, the threesome was pulling into the garage of the Logan ranch. Now, a safe haven for everyone.

Chapter 10
The Hunt for the Assailant
February 2007

*D*oug was in his room, in his mother's converted basement, where he had lived most of his life. It suited him just fine, because he was rarely there. As a freelance photographer, he was often on the road taking pictures, the past several years. He had a walkout door, to the rear of the house, which allowed him access, free from his mother's watchful eyes. They were condemning, inculpatory, blue eyes that physically pierced his skin when she turned them on him. He had always been a burden to her and a hindrance to her lifestyle as a high-priced prostitute. She sent him away to a private school in Europe, when he was five, hoping to be rid of him. He was so badly behaved that he was kicked out of three schools, before she brought him back, at the age twelve. She enrolled him in a private school in NYC, and she made him a suite in the basement of the brownstone she owned. He was to stay out of sight and not cause any trouble.

One of his mother's 'regulars' gave him his first camera. He used to sneak upstairs, when he knew his mother was otherwise occupied, and take candid pictures of her. Doug had drilled a hole into her bedroom wall and hid on the other side with his lens peering through it. He had taken a photography class in school that instructed him on all phases of photography and development. He begged his mother for a darkroom, and she had one made from a closet just off of his bathroom. It was perfect. Doug spent hours perfecting his hobby and learning lessons in life from his mother. He learned to take care of himself and to operate under the radar. As long as his mother didn't have to deal with him, she couldn't have cared less what he was doing.

Doug learned how to blackmail his mother's clients, with his photos. He learned how to post pictures on the Internet and destroyed more than a few marriages. He learned to enjoy having power over others. One day, his mother found out what he had been doing to her clients. She was furious. She tried to throw him out, but he had too much dirt on her. She turned those eyes on him, and he looked for ways to strike back. He wanted her to hurt like he was hurting. He was living up to her projected potential, wasn't he? He began to take out his anger on unsuspecting girls. He used his charm to lure them close and struck out at them, to punish them for their stupidity. He would laugh!" They all were so foolish and deserved what they got. Smilin' Jack was only too happy to show them all how dumb they really were. If Doug's mother suspected what her son was doing, she never came right out and accused him. She insinuated things long before he actually acted them out.

Doug had barely made it home, this time. He had gotten to his friend, the veterinarian, and had the six inch laceration, on his left forearm, stitched up. The vet gave him a shot of antibiotic and wrapped the wound. That was good enough for Doug. He limped home and lay, quietly, in his bed for several days, not wanting his mother to know he was there. He didn't feel up to dealing with her. Not just yet, anyway. All this was her fault, and he would deal with her soon enough. Now he was lying on his bed having just taken some Tylenol. His arm was killing him.

He was listening to the radio. He heard a report on a manhunt for a "serial attacker" responsible for the attack on Emma Masters and several other women over the past twelve years. He perked up. Doug liked the sound of that. It made him feel significant in this insignificant world. "An arrest was imminent."

Like he had never heard that before. They always say that, Doug laughed to himself. *Yet, here I still am.* Then he remembered his camera. He got up from his bed and went to the desk by the door where he had dumped his things when he got home after that last miserable venture. He wasn't ready to call it a failure until he viewed the film. He was aroused with anticipation. He held the camera in both of his hands and pushed the power on button. There the trusting bitch lay, totally unsuspecting. Just enough light from the window to illuminate her oblivious body. *This will be good.* he thought.

Doug was watching the attack so intently he didn't hear his mother descending the carpeted stairs to his rooms. She didn't know he was home until she heard the yelling and the noise from the camcorder. "If it isn't, Dougie, at his most charming self. You in the porno movie business now, Dougie?" She stared at him with those blue eyes, a vodka and orange juice in one hand. She was drinking again. "Maybe I can star in one of your films. I still have what it takes, don't I Dougie?" She dropped her robe to the floor revealing the aging, naked body of a sixty year old, "has been".

"You disgusting slut!" Doug shut off the camera and turned to leave the room.

She strutted towards him. "Don't you think your momma is

still beautiful?" She went to grab his arm.

"Back off, you drunken whore." Doug could feel those eyes boring holes in his back. He swung his good right arm, around back, at his mother to drive her away. Instead he hit the drunken woman on the side of her, all ready, dizzy head. She lost her balance and fell back, hitting the back of her head on the desk. Doug heard a whack—thud, and his mother was lying on the floor. A spreading halo of blood was surrounding her head. "Now look what you've gone and done." He knelt down next to her naked body and tried to rouse her. "Mom, this isn't funny." His dead mother didn't respond. "Well you can't stay here." Doug wrapped his mother in a blanket, pulled her back up the stairs to her bathroom, and rolled her into the bathtub. "You can sleep it off here, in case you get sick." Doug headed back to his room to finish watching his video of Emma. He helped himself to a six pack of beer, from his mother's refrigerator, on his way. His arm was bleeding again after the strenuous work, but he didn't notice. He sat back with his beer and watched the recording over and over, until he finally fell asleep.

Detective Marks was looking at the evidence report from the assault on Emma Masters. She had run the blood samples and they didn't match any known suspects. The finger print from the window wasn't a match either. "How could this guy get away with this behavior for so long and not have been caught for anything? He should be in the system." It was like taking one step forward and three steps back. Then she got the report on the listening device that that body guard alerted her to. That discovery made her look good to her chief. There were two places in the NY city area that sold such a device. She was heading out to see what she could discover at both places. She hoped she would get lucky. David Logan was calling, twice a day, for progress updates. She could hear in his voice that he was at the breaking point.

Rod had the best private investigator he knew looking into the assailant's identity and whereabouts. He had gotten information from David, Emma, and detective Marks and fed that to his PI, Justin Steele. Justin had his own contacts in the New York area and was putting all his focus on finding this guy. Rodney had flown Lora, Melodie, and Emma to Florida. First to Emma's parents, and then the girls spent ten days in Walt Disney World. The suites at the Hilton were perfect. They spent time at the pool and took in the sites at Disney. It was midwinter break so the place was packed. It was hard work for Rod, but the girls were relaxed and having a great time. He wouldn't let anything or anyone interfere with that. He was on edge, waiting to hear from Justin. He had no doubt Justin would find this guy. It was just a matter of time.

David met with a private investigator. The police were not as efficient as he had hoped they would be. They just weren't getting the job done. How could they let a serial, sexual pervert, remain on the loose for so many years, harming so many women? It was a disgrace, and he had had enough. It was time to take matters into his hands. If they weren't motivated to get this guy, he certainly was. He had gotten the name of a private investigator from a friend, from work, who worked with a guy who had suspected his wife of infidelity. The PI was very discreet and thorough. He could locate anyone. However, he needed a name. This was proving to be a problem. If detective Marks had a name, she wasn't revealing that information to David. He would have to find another source in the department. He had made several friends, in the department, over the years that were close to the case. He would talk with them. They will give him the name as soon as one is available. Then he could take care of this, once and for all.

Doug logged onto his computer and went directly to the *Lora Logan fan Club,* web page. It was under "Favorites". There were the usual publicity shots; nothing new there. The same welcome letter from the star; all fairly boring. Doug decided to check some other sites that were notorious for the more candid views of stars. The very sites he used to publish his work. He found a lot of crappy photos, and short film from people's cell phones. Then something caught his eye. It was grainy but it was a picture of Lora and Emma. He knew it was recent, because of the cast on Emma's arm. He examined the photo closer and discovered it was taken at the Disney theme park, on one of the rides. He looked at the date; it was posted, this morning. "I bet those two are still there. I think I could use a little warm weather myself." Doug phoned the airport and reserved a seat on the next direct flight, from La Guardia to Florida. He would be on the 7:00PM flight, so he had plenty of time to get ready. He looked at the clock, only 10:00AM. He showered and re-bandaged his arm. A lightweight, button shirt would be best. He packed a few things in a carry-on duffel bag. He picked up a baseball hat and his sunglasses. This is just what I need, a little vacation. He left by his back entrance and drove to a corner diner for a bite to eat. He had some time to kill, anyway.

Detective Marks struck out at the first shop she went to, but the owner of the second shop remembered selling the listening devise to a man about thirty years old, at the beginning of the month. He gave his description as: sandy haired, clean cut, well dressed and very charming. The man had said he needed it for the office phone, because he suspected someone was giving away company secrets, and he wanted to find out who it was. He paid in cash, but the owner said he may have a picture on his surveillance camera. He recorded over them at the end of each month, and this being only the 23rd,, it was likely the man was captured on tape. He led the detective and her partner to a back office and showed them the tape, one for each week.

Olivia put the first disk into the computer and watched it. After several customers came and went, the owner said, "There! That's him." Olivia looked at her partner and smiled. This was the biggest lead they had so far.

"We'll be taking this with us. Thank you for your cooperation." The owner nodded, and the two cops went back to the station. It wouldn't take long to run a still through the computer files and see if a match pops up anywhere in the country.

Olivia took the surveillance tape, directly to the lab. She wanted a still shot that she could scan into the system. She got it within a few minutes and scanned it in. Little head shots, rapidly flashed before her in succession. It was dizzying to watch so she turned away, knowing the computer would alert her if there was a match. After five minutes the computer made a "Ping", and the words "Match" flashed on the monitor. Underneath the head shot was a brief profile of the individual.

Name: Douglas Allen Civics
Born: February 2, 1975
Address: 25 Remsen St., Brooklyn Heights, NY
Record: voyeurism 1988
shoplifting 1989

Olivia was reading out load to no one in particular. "Looks like a little punk when he was young. A few infractions when he was a minor. Then he must have smartened up. He applied for a job at the college in 1995. They did a small background check and photo ID.

That's when the first attack was reported isn't it?"

Olivia's partner had joined her carrying two cups of coffee. He handed one to Olivia. " Yeah, I think so."

"Look, we have an address here. Let's go check it out; bring Mr. Civics in for questioning." They took their coffees and headed for the car. Olivia was feeling a bit giddy and hopeful.

A policeman, in the vicinity, overheard the conversation and was calling David Logan. He had the name David was waiting for. He even had a photo to fax. He walked to the fax machine while dialing David. "I have something you will be very interested in. Do you have a fax machine?"

"Yes, what do you have?" David asked.

"The jack pot. A picture and name."

"My God, man, both? what's the name?" David could hardly contain his emotions. He was on his feet.

"The name is, Douglas Civics. Give me a fax number and I'll send his picture." He was laying the picture into the scanner as they spoke. David rattled off the number as the officer typed it into the scanner/fax machine. It whirred to life. A few minutes later David told the officer he had it and thanked him very much. David left the construction office with the photo securely in his pocket. He dialed the PI's number and told him to meet at their out-of-the-way spot. He had the information he had been waiting for. If the police didn't get this, Doug Civics, his PI would.

In Florida, the girls were lying by the pool, in their bathing suits, with cold iced teas in their hands. It was 75 degrees, a welcome break from the northern Arizona or New York winters. They were one week into their vacation break and totally at ease. They had some color and looked healthy, except for Emma's cast. She couldn't go into the pool, but enjoyed watching Lora and her daughter play.

They were the only occupants, at the moment, which suited them just fine. Recognized, Lora graciously signed a few autographs, while Emma and Melodie stood in the background. Rodney was always by her side; keeping watch, and never allowing her to stay in one place for long. He was sitting at a table under a shade umbrella, in back of the girls. His laptop was open on the teak table in front of him. His cell phone rang. It was Justin Steele.

Justin was monitoring the police scanner when he heard a call for back up from Detective Marks. He went to the address in Brooklyn Heights. The Detective also called for a coroner. He strolled up and chatted with one of the policemen, obviously a rookie, outside of the building. He was way too talkative. Justin had learned that this was the address of the serial assaulter, and that they found a woman dead in the bathtub. Justin chatted a few more minutes, so as not to be too suspicious. He hoped he was acting very casual, like the other residents in the street. As soon as he could, he went to his car and called Rod.

"The perverts name is Doug Civics. I'm outside of his home as we speak."

"Are you serious? They located him?" Rod tried to hush his excited voice.

"Hold on. They didn't find him here. What they found was a dead woman in a bathtub. He's on the run. I'll track him down though."

"Keep me updated. I want to know what direction he's headed." Rod hung up.

Justin was on his way to the airport with a photo he had gotten from the rookie. The police were also headed to the bus, train and airport, also armed with the same photo. There was only one of him, but he had pretty good instincts, and his instincts were telling him to go to the airport. At La Guardia, he checked for the latest flights out and went to those boarding gates. He flashed a badge and was allowed free access. The fourth gate was a flight to Florida. Justin hoped he would strike out here, but the man at the desk recognized the man in the photo. Justin called Rodney back.

Rodney was still keeping vigil over the girls at the pool when his phone rang, again.

"I have a picture. He's headed your way." That was all Justin had to say. Where and when would this guy show up?

"Fax me the picture." Rodney hung up the phone and went to Lora's chair, she was toweling off her hair. "Lora, are you girls ready to head up to the room?"

"As a matter of fact we are. Do you have to use the little boy's room?" she teased. She noticed the serious look on his face. "What's wrong Rod?" she asked, concerned.

"Let's go on up." He turned to Emma and Melodie. "We're heading up to the suite, now, if that's all right with everyone." He attempted a weak smile.

The girls didn't notice but Lora knew him better. She was feeling anxious.

Once back in their suite Melodie went to shower to get dressed. Emma went to the kitchenette to get a snack. Rod told them all to stay put while he went to his suite. He wanted to get the picture that Justin had faxed him. He had to get a look at this animal. He was looking at the picture when Lora walked into the room. He tried to flip it over and lay it on the desk, before Lora got a look at it.

"What's that? What's going on Rod?"

"We got a name and picture." He spoke with quiet control.

Lora stood frozen to the floor. She blinked her eyes, but couldn't speak. Rod took a step toward her and wrapped his ever-protective arms around her. He spoke softly in her ear. "His name is Doug Civics."

"Do they have him in custody, then?"

"No. He left before they got to him."

"Of course he did. It's not over."

"Not yet, No."

She pushed back from Rod and looked up into his eyes. "What were you looking at when I came in?" Rod tried to draw her close but she pushed back on his flexed biceps. "What?"

"It's a picture of Doug Civics."

"May I see it?"

"Are you sure?"

"I'll let you know if it is my attacker or not."

Rod reached over to the desk and flipped the paper over to reveal the picture. He held onto Lora with his left arm Lora put her hand over her mouth to stifle an utterance of painful recognition. Rod quickly flipped the paper over to hide the image and put both arms around the weeping Lora. Her face was buried in his massive chest. He had his answer. *This was the guy, and he will pay.*

Doug had landed in Orlando, rented a compact car, and drove south to Kissimmee. There, he got a room at a Days Inn. He wasted no time unpacking his laptop to look for any new information on Lora Logan. *Ahh, a sighting at the Hilton in Disney World.* Doug set about assembling the ingredients he had purchased at a local drug store and put the devise in his camera bag. He changed into a light-weight flowered shirt that he hoped would make him fit in as a tourist. He grabbed his camera bag and headed to the theme park. He had a plan.

David Logan had discovered, from his PI, that Doug Civics

was headed to Florida. He too was boarding a flight to go there. He thanked the PI and said he would take it from there. He called Rodney to let him know that he was on his way.

Rod's phone rang. He pulled it from his pocket, with his right hand, while still holding Lora close. It was David Logan.

"Hey Rod, just wanted to let you know I'm getting on a plane for Florida in thirty minutes. I learned that maniac is headed that way."

"I have the same information." Rod told him. "I suspect he's all ready here." He watched Lora lift her head and took at him with wide eyes. This was the first she was learning this news.

"Is that my father?" she asked.

Rod nodded the affirmative. She held her hand out for the phone. "Daddy?"

"Hi, baby. I'll be there in a few hours. You girls sit tight with Rod. He'll take good care of you."

Emma came to the open doorway. She sensed the tension in the room and saw the serious looks on Lora and Rod's faces. "Hey guys, what's going on?"

"He's here!" Lora simply stated.

"Where, exactly? In the hotel?" Emma asked, wide eyed and frightened.

Rod answered, "In Florida. I think he'll come to the park. I'd like you all to stay in the suite until I make arrangements to fly you back to the ranch. Lora's father will be here in a few hours. He is terribly concerned for you girls. The good news is, the police know who this maniac is and have a picture. They have an all points bulletin out on him. I am going to alert the hotel security, now. He isn't invisible any longer."

Just then Melodie came into the room. "Making plans for

dinner? I'm starving!"

Lora tried to lighten the mood. "You're always starving. Poppa has decided to come and join us for a day or so. We'll sit tight until he gets here."

"Wow! That's a surprise. Is Momma with him?"

"No, apparently Poppa had to meet someone down here, for work, and decided to stay with us," she lied. Soon she would tell Melodie everything. This was not the time. She was still too young at nine.

Rod's phone rang. It was Justin. "He rented a car at the airport two hours ago. I'm there now."

"Thanks, buddy. Would you hang out there for awhile? David Logan will be landing in a couple of hours. You can give him a ride here. I'll call and get his flight number and get back to you," Rod instructed. Lora heard Rod's end of the conversation, but wasn't sure to whom he was talking. She decided to help out by calling her father, for the information Rod needed. Once she relayed it to Rod, he called Justin back with it.

"Melodie, how about relaxing, before dinner,with a movie?" Emma suggested.

"OK. What shall we watch?" Melodie walked into the girl's suite with Emma close behind.

"I'll bet there's a good Disney movie available." They both laughed, considering where they were. Emma pulled the door shut behind her, with her good arm.

Rodney reached for a stray piece of hair that had fallen into Lora's face, gently picking it up and moving it to the side. "It's all going to be okay. I know I keep saying that."

"Why would he come here, when everyone is looking for him?" she asked.

"Maybe he doesn't realize that, yet. They found a body at his house."

Lora looked grim. "Who was it?"

"I'm not sure yet. My PI has been busy trailing, this Doug. Might be something on the news."

Rod turned on the 32" plasma TV, in his room. He tuned to an all-news, all-the-time channel. Lora was still standing by the desk. Rodney was by the TV cabinet, holding the remote control. He backed up to sit down on the edge of the bed to watch. He looked over at Lora standing all alone and looking so vulnerable. He patted the bed beside him. "Come and have a seat."

"Yeah, sure." She sat next to Rod and they watched a lot of local news before some national items were covered. Then what they were waiting for came on: "A high end brothel keeper, 'Angel ' Civics, was found dead in her home. Her son, Douglas Civics, is being sought for questioning. Ms. Civics had been thought to have operated a brothel in the Brooklyn area for many years, while servicing many prominent clients. She left behind a client book which is in the custody of the police." Lora looked at Rodney. "His mother?"

"Apparently. I wonder how she died?"

"I am going to call Detective Marks. I'm surprised we haven't heard from her yet." Lora punched the number on her phone. "Shouldn't she be letting me know what's going on?"

"Hi, Lora. I was just going to call you. We have a huge break in your case." Olivia paused. Lora waited for her to continue, not wanting her to know she knew anything. "We have the name of your assailant. We should have him in custody soon."

"If you know who it is why isn't he in custody now?" Lora asked.

"When we got to his address, he wasn't there. We found his mother in the bathtub. I don't know if you've seen any news reports."

"Was she murdered?"

"We're waiting for the coroner's report. But it looks suspicious. Douglas, that's her son's name, was not there. We put out an all points bulletin on him, as a person of interest. When we get him, we'll interrogate him on the assault cases, too. We're collecting evidence at the home and processing it. I'll keep you informed."

"Do you know where he is now?" Lora asked.

"We have reason to believe he has headed to Florida."

"Do you realize that I'm in Florida, now, with my sister, and Emma? Do you think that he knows we're here?"

"We don't know what he's thinking, to be honest. We'll get him, though. It's just a matter of time. Do you have enough security with you, Lora?" Olivia was concerned, also.

"Rodney will take care of things, here. Just catch him, please," Lora pleaded. She hung up. "She doesn't know anymore than we do." Lora sounded disappointed and discouraged. She turned to Rod, who was talking on his phone.

He held up a finger to tell Lora "just a moment OK, I alerted the hotel security. There's someone posted at all entrances to this floor: elevators and stairwells. They have a description, but I asked for someone to come to my room to get some photos. I printed up some copies to be handed out."

Just then, there was a light knock on the door. Lora jumped. "Security here." came from the other side of the door. Rod went to the door and peeked through the peep hole. A uniformed man with dark hair and dark eyes was standing on the other side. Rod opened the door, slightly, and handed the man the pile of photos.

"Thank you." he said. "See that all the staff, on all shifts, has a look at these."

"Yes Sir." The man said.

Rod closed and locked the door. "I guess we sit and wait for your father."

Lora went to Rod and gave him a hug. "Thanks for everything. I couldn't manage without you."

"You don't have to." He slid his dark hands up and down her lightly tanned arms. It made goosebumps raise on them. He smiled, inside, to know he had that effect on her. He had grown very fond of Lora, over the past year he had been protecting her. He knew he shouldn't, but he couldn't help himself. He has wanted to kiss her for a long time, but he had great restraint. It came from years of professionalism and training. He would wait for a sign from Lora.

Lora could hear the movie in the next room. She could hear Emma talking to Mel. What a wonderful friend she had in Emma. What a wonderful friend she had in Rod. She felt so loved at this moment; even with uncertainty and imminent danger threatening them. All Lora could think about was Rod's powerful arms holding her. "How long before my father gets here?" she asked Rod, as she entwined her fingers with his and laid her forehead on his solid chest.

"Lora." He whispered in her ear. Dare he hope that Lora had feelings other than friendship for him? *'Calm down, she is turning to you because she is frightened, and nothing more you fool.* He thought to himself. *You're the professional here. Don't take advantage of the situation. How easy that would be.* He cleared his throat. " Umm, Justin said he would call when your father's plane landed. Can I get anything for you, or the girls, while we wait?" he finally spit out, while still holding Lora's hands in his.

"What I need... is you Rod." She pulled his hands up and held them to her chest.

Rod sighed at the feel of her heart beating so fast. "Not now, baby. Maybe when this whole mess is behind you ... well ...you may feel differently."

"I understand. You aren't attracted to me, because of my past." She looked so sad.

"Oh, that's not it at all. Your past has helped to make you the beautiful woman you are. I love the woman I see." He pushed her back and held her delicate face in his strong hands. "It is taking every ounce of strength in me not to pick you up and carry you to that bed." He kissed her, then, for the first time. He kissed her eye lids, her cheeks, lips, hot neck, and shoulders.

Lora rolled her head back and welcomed the long awaited kisses. She sighed. "I don't want to wait."

"Oh God, baby. I don't think you are thinking clearly." He continued to kiss her neck and brought her hands to his moist lips. "I know **I'm** not this very moment. You're driving me mad."

"I'm thinking very clearly. Who knows what tomorrow will bring? All we really have is the here and now." She reached on her tip toes to kiss Rod again on his moist lips.

"We shouldn't. I shouldn't. We have a working relationship. I don't want to ruin that." He couldn't resist her warm kisses. She smelled of coconut suntan lotion, from her afternoon at the pool. Her hair was still slightly damp as he entwined his fingers in it to pull her head closer to his face.

"I've never been with a man, Rod. I've never wanted to, until now, that is." She was unbuttoning his shirt. She slipped it off his broad shoulders, down his back and arms. Laying her face on his hard, muscular shoulder she said, "Please, I've grown to love you."

She reached behind her back and unfastened her bathing suit top, letting it fall to the floor between them.

Rod pulled her close so that her naked breasts pressed against his naked chest and whispered in her ear, " Do you know how long I've waited to hear you say that?" He pushed her back slightly to look into her eyes. "I have loved you since that day in your agent's office. The day you got that horrid phone call." His lips brushed her face softly like the wings of a butterfly. "I love your strength, your beauty, your devotion to family."

"And I could say the same about you. I love your gentle soul, and big heart."

"Ah, Lora. You are so young, and confused. You are so beautiful." He kissed her bare shoulders and cupped her naked breasts in his warm hands.

"Not about this. I know how I feel. I've been waiting my whole life to feel like this. To be with a man that I'm not afraid to have touch me." She sighed at his intimate touch.

Rod picked Lora up off her feet in one easy movement. He held her in his arms and carried her to the bed. He laid her down as gently as a baby. "I don't want to do anything to hurt you."

"I'm not as fragile as my father believes I am. I'm ready for this." She pulled Rod down to her and kissed him. After they made love they lay breathless under the sheets, Lora laid with her head on Rods chest, with his arm around her. She was tracing abstract patterns lightly on his hairless chest. They heard the credits playing on the TV in the other room. " We'd better get dressed. The movie is done. They may come looking for us." Lora gave Rod another kiss before getting out of bed. She gathered up her bathing suit and went into the bathroom.

Rod lay there a minute longer, wondering if it was all a beautiful dream. Could this beautiful girl really love him? Then he was pulled back to reality when his cell phone rang. Justin was calling to say David's plane had landed and they were on their way. Rod thanked him for the heads up. He got out of bed just as Lora was walking out of the bathroom in his bathrobe. "Your dad's plane has landed and he'll be here soon."

"I guess I'd better get dressed. May we continue this another time?" she teased, kissing him before he went into the bathroom. Lora went to her room to get dressed. Rod took a quick shower and dressed in light weight, tan pants and buttoned, short sleeve shirt. He knocked on the girl's door to see if they needed anything. Emma said, "Come in." She was looking at him with a broad smile across her face.

"What?" He asked.

"Oh, nothing." She answered, still smiling. "Lora will be right out."

"I was wondering if you needed anything? Mr. Logan is on his way from the airport. We can have some dinner sent up if you're hungry."

"I'm still starving!" Melodie announced.

Lora came out of the bathroom dressed in a white sun-dress trimmed in gold, that made her new tan look very dark. She looked like a goddess and was stunning with her dark, wavy hair, falling around her shoulders. It was in stark contrast with the dress. Her face had a natural rosiness to her cheeks. Rod couldn't take his eyes off of her. She had never looked so lovely. Emma shook her head and smiled at him. Lora had to smile, herself, at his "gaga" stare. He looked like a schoolboy standing there. That's the effect she was going for. Mission accomplished! She looked over at Emma and winked. They knew each other so well, they didn't need words.

"I...ummm..I was just...ah.." Rod stammered.

"Yes Rod?" Lora said walking over to him. She could smell his freshly applied aftershave and inhaled deeply.

He inhaled her freshly soaped skin. So natural and fresh.

"Yes. I was just about to order something for dinner. Your father will be hungry when he gets here." He took a big breath, happy to have gotten out what he wanted to say.

"Sounds like a plan. I know that Mel and Emma are hungry, and I'm ravenous." She smiled at him.

"Good." He paused and looked? at her. "Good" he repeated. "Then that's what we'll do." He slapped his hands together in an attempt to pull himself back to the business at hand.

Lora came to his rescue by going to the phone and dialing room service. "Well, what does everyone want, then?' Lora asked holding the phone to her ear.

Emma answered first. "I could go for a turkey club sandwich!"

Melodie piped up, "Pizza for me!"

"I think turkey sounds great." Lora added. "What about you Rod?"

"I could go for a med-rare juicy steak, I guess." The girls all looked at him.

"Worked up an appetite by the pool today, Rod?" Emma winked at Lora when she asked.

Even with Rod's dark skin, Lora could see him blush. *How endearing,* she thought to herself. "I'll order one for my father and your friend, also." Lora called in the order.

Chapter 11
The Abduction
February 2007

All of a sudden the fire alarms went off. Rod and Lora stood there looking at each other, not sure what was going on. Melodie rushed to her mother's side. "What's going on?" she yelled, over the noise of the fire alarm. They could hear people running in the hallway.

"I'm not sure, but don't move, just yet." Rod was about to call the front desk when he heard someone pounding on his door.

"Mr. Blackman, We have to evacuate the hotel! There has been an explosion!" The pounding continued. "Mr. Blackman! This is security! Please have your party evacuate the building!"

Rod hurried to the door and opened it slightly, looking out at the chaos in the hall. He didn't see smoke, but he closed the door quickly and turned to the two women and Melodie, who were awaiting his instructions. "Looks like we have to leave with the other guests. I want us to stick close together. We'll go to the gazebo by the pool. If we get split up, by any chance, plan to meet there."

"I want to grab my purse and cell phone." Emma went back

into her room to get them. "I'll get your purse, Lora, it's right here." She returned seconds later and handed Lora her purse.

"Thanks Emma." Lora accepted the purse from her and felt her pocket in her dress for her phone. "I'm all set."

Emma took ahold of Melodie's left hand with her good right hand. Lora took hold of Melodie's right hand and they followed Rod out of the door. Rod led the way to the stairwell and held the door open for the girls so they could descend the steps. The lower they went , the smokier it became. Rod took off his shirt and told Melodie to put it over her face. Emma let go of Melodie in order to cover her mouth and nose with her right hand. Rod urged them to hurry down and get to the gazebo. Emma reached the ground floor first. Someone was holding the door open, allowing everyone to head straight for the open lobby doors. She knew the way to the pool. The lobby was full of people pushing their way out. Rod took hold of Lora and was almost pulling her along to the exit.

Lora's hand slipped off Melodie's; she stopped short. "Mel, where are you? Rod! I lost Mel." People were pushing her from all sides. She felt Rod's grip on her arm. But she didn't have hold of Melodie. Then she heard her not far away.

"I'm here!" Melodie called.

"Get outside!" Rod ordered. "We can see clearer there. Less smoke," he coughed.

"I don't see Emma." Lora said. " Don't see Mel." She was beginning to panic.

"I see Emma, just outside the door. Look!" Rod told her.

Lora coughed. "Melodie, are you here?" Lora called again, reaching out for her daughter.

"I'm just behind you. I see you. I can't reach your hand." Melodie answered.

"Rod can you grab hold of Mel?"

Rod was still holding Lora's arm. Mel was slightly to the right and rear of Lora. Rod reached out for her when someone slammed into him making him shove Lora out the door and knocking her to the ground. Rod pulled her to her feet and asked her if she was hurt.

"No, I'm fine. Where's Mel? Did you get her?" she asked, looking around.

Emma rushed up to them. "Everyone make it out? Where's Mel?"

Everyone was looking around. They all called her name. "MELODIE!" They were coughing slightly and turning this way and that, to check in all directions. There were many people around them running in different directions, and so much noise and confusion, that no one spotted her. Lora grabbed Emma's right arm and stood close to her. Rod was taller than the two women and looked over their heads, as the crowd pouring from the hotel thinned. Then he spotted something on the ground, near the door. He wanted a closer look.

"Walk this way." He pulled them towards the door that they had just exited. His shirt was lying on the pavement, trampled. He stooped to pick it up. Lora looked first at the shirt and then at Rodney, standing there, in his white sleeveless tee shirt. "It's my shirt she was using. Good she made it out. We'd better head to the gazebo to see if she is there."

They rushed through the crowd that was now milling about in confusion. They headed to the designated meeting spot. Smoke was pouring from many windows. The firefighters were uncoiling their hoses and rushing inside the hotel with them. Rod stopped one of them and told them that he was looking for a nine-year-old girl. He thought she might have gotten out, but wasn't positive. They would be on the alert for her inside. "We had better get to the gazebo. She may be scared if we aren't there." They hurried around back to the pool area. There were quite a few people gathered there. Rod scanned the crowd for any sign of Melodie. They reached the gazebo but Melodie still was nowhere in sight.

"OH, MY GOD!" Where can she be? I hope she isn't injured!" Lora cried. She was franticly looking for her daughter around the crowded pool area, from her spot in the gazebo that Rod held her in. He didn't want her running around in the crowd. All Lora could do was call her name. "MELODIE!" she shouted. She called her name over and over. Lora was shaking with fear, now.

People turned in her direction and starred. Then people started to recognize her. Some took pictures with their cell phones. Many pushed closer to get a better look at the celebrity. They were curious about what she was shouting about. Rod tried to place himself between the people and Lora to shield her from their prying eyes. She looked a sight in her smoke stained, white dress and tear streaked sooty face.

Emma grabbed Lora by her arm and turned her so they were face to face. "She's here somewhere. We'll find her."

"Of course she is." Lora took a breath. "She has to be. Oh God please. She has to be."

Rod's cell phone rang. He answered abruptly, "Yeah." It was Justin calling from the front of the hotel; wondering what was going on. "Evacuation. Some kind of explosion I guess. We are in back, by the pool. David Logan with you?"

The pair was rounding the corner. Lora spotted her father coming toward her.

"Oh Daddy!" Rod stepped aside to allow David room to hold

his daughter. "Thank God you're here. We can't find Mel," she sobbed.

Rod was talking to Justin in hushed voices. Justin nodded and went back to the front of the hotel. He would find out how this explosion happened and look for Melodie.

"Thank God you girls are safe." David hugged Emma, then.

"Daddy, we lost sight of Mel just inside the hotel."

David looked to Rodney. "Where is Melodie?"

"We're not sure yet, sir." He held up the shirt Melodie was using to shield her face from the smoke. "We found this just outside the door, on the sidewalk." He explained to David how Melodie was using it to cover her face. "We assume she made it out. This was our designated meeting spot, in case we got separated."

"You lost her?" David yelled. People were, again, looking in their direction. A hotel security guard was walking towards them. Rodney recognized him from his dealing with security, for Lora.

"Glad to see you made it out safely." He smiled at Lora, like any other star struck fan.

"We have a problem." Rod tried to talk quietly so that on-lookers wouldn't overhear.

"Miss Logan and her sister got separated in the evacuation. Have you seen the nine-year-old girl?"

"That cute little girl with dark hair and blue eyes? I remember her. No I haven't seen her. I'll alert the hotel personnel to look for her, though. I'm sure she's here somewhere." He tipped his hat at Lora and smiled.

"This was to be our meeting spot, if we got separated, but she hasn't shown up yet. Could you have someone stay here and wait for her? Rod asked the guard. I want to take Miss Logan and her friend to a more secure area."

"No problem, Mr. Blackman. You should take Miss Logan to the hotel office."

"Thank you for all of your help." Rod turned back to his group. "Mr. Logan would you and the girls follow me. We are getting out of this crowd."

"We can't leave. What if Melodie is looking for us?" Lora protested, peeling his hand off her arm.

"This guard is going to wait here. Let's go. It's too crowded here."

"I agree with Rodney. We had better go with him," David encouraged. The crowd around them was growing and starting to clamor for autographs. David took Lora by the arm and Rod took Emma. Rod led the way back, inside, to the office that the guard had indicated. They were expecting the small group, and ushered them through a door behind the registration desk, quickly, and closed the door, leaving the pandemonium outside.

The hotel manager knocked and entered. "Miss Logan, I am so sorry to inconvenience you and your party this way. If there is anything we can do, please let anyone at the hotel know. We are so honored to have you staying with us."

"What exactly happened here?" Rod asked.

"There was some sort of an explosion just outside of the kitchen door, filling the kitchen with smoke, which set off the smoke alarm. In the confusion and surprise, one of the kitchen staff spilled some grease causing a fire which set off the sprinklers. Your suites, however, are unharmed and you may return to them if you would like, the manager told them.

"That's all well and good, but my daughter is still unaccounted for." David spoke up, now.

"The whole staff is searching the premises for her. The police have been called. If you would like to return to your rooms, we will keep you informed. I think you will be more comfortable there."

"I think that's an excellent idea, Lora." Rod said. "Melodie knows her way there."

"Yes, Of course you're right. We should wait for her there." Lora agreed

"David, if you would escort the girls to their room, I have some things to check out. I want to find Justin and see what he has learned. I'll be up soon." He touched Lora's arm and gave it a slight squeeze as a comforting gesture. She understood and pleaded to him with her eyes. He understood. She was right, earlier. You never do know what will happen tomorrow, or the next minute for that matter.

David took hold of each girl by an arm and walked to the elevator. The firemen had cleared the hoses from the lobby, and the hotel cleaning crew were busy cleaning up. People were returning to their rooms. Some had gathered their baggage and were checking out. The threesome was alone in the elevator for the ride to their floor. They met a chamber maid, with her fully equipped cart, outside of their room. "Miss Logan, your suite is ready." She opened the door with her pass key.

"Thank you." Lora said, softly, and walked inside followed by Emma and her father. Once inside, in the privacy of her room, Lora broke down and cried. Her father went to her trying to comfort her. "Daddy, what could have happened to my baby?"

"We're going to find her. She can't be far." Emma said.

Lora's phone rang. "Mimi?" Melodie was quiet and reserved, totally unlike her usual bubbly personality.

"BABY! Where are you?" Lora asked, excitedly. "We have been looking all over the hotel for you."

Then there came a different voice. "Baby is fine. Baby is mighty fine." Lora recognized the voice and collapsed into the nearby chair. Her father was watching her with concern He mouthed the word, "What?"

"Don't you touch her!" Lora yelled into the phone, holding it, now, with two shaking hands.

"She has the prettiest blue eyes." The line went dead. Lora screamed and fainted. Emma ran to her aid.

David was calling Rod. "Get up here to the room, NOW!" He hung up and went to Lora. Emma got a cold drink of water and brought it to David, who, now, had Lora in his arms. Lora opened her eyes, and David helped her back into the chair. Minutes later Rod was running through the door, followed by Justin "That bastard has Melodie!" David yelled.

Rod looked at Lora slumped in the chair. Tears were still running down her dirty face. Rod went to her and squatted down in front, putting his hands on her knees. "Tell me what happened."

"She just called me." She accepted a tissue from Rod. "He said," Lora had to pause.

"she has pretty blue eyes. He knows, I know he does." She wiped the tears from her face.

Rod laid his head on the side of her face, tenderly. "We'll find her. We'll get her back." Rod stood and went to Justin, who was standing next to David. Emma went to Lora, put her arm around her, and handed her the water. The men were talking softly. "Justin, let's bring David up to speed on what we know so far."

"Yeah, sure. I showed the picture of Doug around. A kitchen employee saw him in the alleyway, behind the kitchen, minutes before the explosion. He was wearing a hotel bellhop uniform." Justin looked at his notes a minute. "This guy rented a black, Ford Fiesta at the airport. I have given the plate number to the police."

"Can the police issue an Amber alert?" David asked.

"I'll call the local authorities now." Justin moved aside to call and make the report.

"Do we know where he is staying?" David asked.

"Not yet. The police are canvassing motels and hotels in the area. It will take some time. He hasn't used any credit cards, except to rent the car." Justin told him.

David was clearly agitated. "What the hell are we suppose to do?"

"You need to stay here with Lora. Maybe he'll contact her again. I'll see if the police can trace any calls to her cell phone." Rod said

Justin had finished his call. "They are sending some detectives over to make out a report."

Chapter 12
The Wrong Logan
8:00 PM

Doug had decided, in his motel room, earlier that day, that he wanted Lora Logan for himself. He wanted to bring the "up-and-coming star" back down to earth. *Who did she think she was, anyway?* He devised a mental plan as to how he would accomplish that. Doug found a laundry room that happened to have bellhop uniforms hanging on a rack. *Nice of this place to launder the employee's uniforms. Convenient, too.* He put on a uniform that was his size and left the room. Step two in his plan; plant the little explosive devise he had made. He walked around the hotel and decided on the kitchen exit. He wasn't out to hurt anyone, just evacuate the hotel so he could get next to Lora. He heard on the news that the police wanted him "for questioning." He was a "person of interest" in the death of his mother. "They were so stupid. She wasn't dead. *They don't know what a drama queen she is. She knows how to work people."*

"*All women like to play their games. They are so pathetic. They think we men don't see them for what they are. Liars and players,all of them.*

This Lora Logan is one of the biggest game players. Thinks she is so special. Not for much longer. I'll take care of her, put her back in her place, the little tramp."

Doug had gone to a drug store and gotten sulfur, sugar and potassium nitrate to make some gun powder. He planted the explosive devise he had thrown together, next to the dumpster. It was sure to make an immense noise and cause a great deal of commotion with the amount of white smoke it would create. They would think it was a fire for sure. Now Doug planted himself by the stairway door to watch for *her.*

He heard the explosion. *Right on time.*

People were running from the back of the hotel. Someone yelled "FIRE!" This was working perfectly. Panic was overtaking the guests and staff. The kitchen staff was running to the front of the hotel, He heard the fire alarms going off. He was smiling. Guests and housekeeping staff began to come down the stairs because the elevators had been shut down. He stood and held the door open and watched. This was the closest exit from her room. He'd found that out from a stupid housekeeping broad that he used his charm on.

He saw security people in black uniforms heading to the upper floors. He knew it would be their job to make sure the building was evacuated. It won't be long, now. He heard the fire trucks pulling up, one in back and one in front. Employees were escorting someone who was coughing from the smoke. He couldn't believe the amount of smoke. It was starting to spill into the lobby. People were running with clothing over their eyes and mouths. He never dreamed it would make so much smoke. Something else must have happened. He grew concerned that he might not be able to see *her,* if the smoke got any thicker. A steady stream of guests was pouring out through the front doors from all directions, within the hotel. It was total havoc. It was becoming harder for Doug to breath. *Come on!, move it you dumb broad,* he was thinking to himself. Then they came, past him, through the door. He followed closely behind, looking for his chance to grab Lora. That big goon was always in the way. He gave him a shove with his shoulder, and he almost fell on top of Lora. *Shit, that didn't work.*

He grabbed hold of the little girls arm. She had her head covered. "Right this way Little Missy." Doug pretended to help her out. Melodie could see the familiar uniformed arm from under her makeshift veil. She knew he worked for the hotel so she let the uniformed man lead her to safety. Melodie heard Lora call for her and answered back. She saw that they had made it onto the sidewalk outside and pulled the shirt from her head. She didn't see Lora, Emma, or Mr. Rod anywhere. There were so many people running around, and firemen and police were trying to help them. The man was pulling her further away from everyone.

"I'm suppose to meet Mimi in the gazebo, by the pool." She said to the man. She was trying to get free from him. In the distance, now, she heard Lora call her name, again. Just as she was about to answer, the man put his hand over her mouth, picked her off the ground at her waist, and began to run. Now, Melodie was frightened. She tried to yell at the man who was carrying her. Her words were muffled. She was kicking and even tried to bite his hand.

Doug ran to his parked car and threw Melodie into the hot trunk, slamming the trunk lid shut. *Shit,* He didn't want the kid. He had to think. *Lora will come for the kid. This may still work.* He thought. *Now, where should I go? This place will be swarming with cops soon.* It was getting late.

Doug decided to head back to his room, but to leave the car in a parking lot, somewhere. He had used a credit card to get the car. They must know about that. But he paid cash for the room. He'd sneak the kid in under cover of dark, and no one would know.

Doug drove back to the Days Inn. He parked the car behind a restaurant. He popped the trunk release. The girl was crying and soaked in sweat. "Get out." Doug said firmly. He pulled her roughly by her arm. She whimpered in pain. That made Doug smile. Once she was standing behind the car Doug gave her a tug, "Let's go." He slammed the trunk lid down and headed in the direction of the motel. He stayed out of sight as much as possible. Luckily, his room was in the back. They walked up the outside steps to the balcony that ran the length of building. Doug was practically dragging Melodie along, now. His room was five doors down. They didn't meet a soul. Many of the rooms on this side seemed unoccupied. Most guests opted for the rooms on the inside, overlooking the pool.

Doug unlocked the door and pushed the child inside, quickly, before closing and locking the door. He made sure the curtains were drawn tight before turning on the light. Now he was looking at Melodie, for the first time, up close. She stared back at him, with those eyes. He couldn't stop looking at her. She was the spitting image of Lora, but those eyes. *His mother's eyes. His eyes.* He began laughing. He went to one of the double beds and sat down.

Melodie was getting nervous. She was afraid to move or speak. Who was this man, and why was he laughing? Very meekly, she said, "I want to go home." The man was still laughing. When he finally stopped, Melodie asked. "Please, can I go home now?" She wiped the sweat from her brow with her hand. "Can I have a drink?"

"Well, you're just full of questions, now aren't you? Why don't we just call Lora. You do you know her phone number?" Melodie just nodded. Doug pulled the cell phone from his pocket. It was one of those prepaid disposable ones, "Here, call her."

Melodie took the phone and said "Thank you," to Doug. She punched in some numbers and put the phone to her little ear. She was smiling, now, as the phone rang. When Lora answered, Melodie could only say "Mimi?" before the man snatched back the phone. He was smiling. Maybe this was some kind of joke. He didn't talk long. "Is Mimi coming?" She asked.

"NO, she can't come yet." He put the phone back into his pocket.

"But I'm hungry, and we are having dinner with poppa."

"Who is poppa?" he asked her.

"My poppa, David Logan," she answered.

Doug started laughing again. "This is priceless. Talk about games."

"Who are you?" Melodie asked.

"Why don't you just call me... Smilin' Jack. That's what Lora use to call me." He was smiling now.

"Are you friends with my sister?" She used the term sister, out of habit, with strangers.

Doug roared again. "Your sister? You think Lora is your sister?"

"Well I'm supposed to say that, and she's famous now." Melodie smiled for the first time with pride.

"Yes, I know who Lora Logan is. It's too bad that you don't."

Melodie was confused by what the man had just said. "I'm hungry. And," she repeated, "thirsty."

"Well we can't have Lora Logan's 'sister' going hungry can we." He removed his belt and pulled Melodie roughly to the desk chair. "Sit!" He pushed the frightened girl down onto the seat and pulled her arms back. He secured them, behind her, to the chair with his belt.

"Now, if you sit tight and be very quiet, I'll get something for us to eat.

The terrified girl nodded her head affirmatively.

Doug looked at her a minute. "Sorry, can't take any chances." He picked up the pillow from the bed and removed the pillow case. He used it for a gag. "Be a good girl! I'll be right back." He smiled at her. Her eyes were huge. They were looking straight at him. Just like his mother's. He had to get out of that room, and now.

Doug remember passing a convenience store earlier in the day. He walked, using the time to clear the image of his mother's eyes from his brain. He realized that he still had on that stupid uniform. He had to lose it before being seen. He took off the jacket and tossed it into the first dumpster he passed. The black pants weren't too bad. Pretty generic. He needed to get rid of the shirt though. He tossed that into the dumpster as well. He was left wearing his white tee shirt and black pants. *This will do,* he thought to himself. Doug was happy he had remembered to bring his sunglasses. Even though it was dark he would wear them in the store. He had learned years ago to keep his eyes covered. People always commented on them. He wished he had a hat, but he forgot to bring his cap.

Once inside the store, he moved quickly. He picked a six pack of cold beer, and one of soda. Then he picked up a box of donuts, a bag of chips, and two hot dogs. He paid for them with cash and headed back to the room. He unlocked the door and Melodie was still sitting quietly in the chair, where he left her. He set the food on the desk and went back to lock the door. "I hope you like hot dogs," Doug said, as he took the gag off of her mouth and removed the belt from her arms. He turned her chair around to face the desk, with Melodie still seated. He set a hot dog and cold soda out for her. "Eat!" he told her. Doug went to sit on the bed behind her. He didn't want to see her eyes while he ate. He turned on the TV, for noise. A special news announcement was on. Oh, what luck. "The fire at the Hilton at Disney." Doug turned up the volume, just a bit, in order to hear above his chewing.

He could see people running from the building. Smoke was billowing up behind it and coming out of the open sets of double doors, in front. Then they put up a picture of the now, famous Lora Logan and went on to report that she was a guest of the hotel, and she and her family had escaped injury.

This caught Melodies attention and she strained to hear the reporter. She didn't dare turn around to look. Doug hadn't noticed because he was looking at the picture of Lora so intently. *Maybe they're coming to get her,* she hoped. She chewed her hot dog and listened.

The next image on the screen was of Doug. He was wanted in New York for questioning in the death of his mother and the abduction of nine-year-old Melodie Logan. Melodie was last seen with her family, at the Hilton, minutes before the explosion. His name was linked with the famous Lora Logan. *Awesome!* Doug was pleased. He had gotten the wrong Logan, but this might work, anyway.

She wasn't sure what abduction meant, but she understood this man's mother was dead, and they knew she was with him.

"I think we should give Miss Lora Logan another call. Don't you Melodie?" Doug wiped his mouth on the back of his hand and took a long drink from the beer bottle.

"Can I go home now?" Melodie ask, innocently, hoping that's why they were phoning. Maybe he was scared because they knew he had her.

"I guess that all depends on your...sister,"he chuckled softly.

Doug handed the phone to Melodie and told her to dial. She did as she was told. He held the phone to her ear.

When Lora answered, Melodie said, "I want to come home now, Mimi." There were no tears from the brave little girl. Of course she had no way of knowing who she was with and what Doug was capable of.

Doug put the phone to his ear. "If you want the kid, you'll have to meet me. We'll do this again the right way." He hung up. He knew what he was going to do now. He pulled the desk chair out with Melodie on it. "Come on kid, we are going on a little road trip to meet your *sister.*" That term made him smile. He finished his beer in one gulp. Doug began gathering up everything from his room. He grabbed Melodie by the arm.

"I have to use the bathroom!" she said quickly.

"Hurry it up." Doug let go of her arm, and she went into the bathroom and closed the door. Doug listened at the door. He knew there was no way out but back through the door she entered.

Melodie really did have to use the bathroom. She also wanted to leave a clue for anyone looking for her. She took off her new Mickey Mouse bracelet and left it on the sink. She wasn't sure if it would help find her, but at least Lora and poppa would know she had been here and was thinking of them. She tried to stall. She washed her hands. Doug yelled "Hurry up kid!" from the other room. She opened the door. Doug was waiting for her. He took hold of her arm so tightly that she knew she would have a bruise there. He pulled her along, almost running back to the car. Once at the car she was sure she would be put into that dark, hot trunk, and she was afraid. But Doug surprised her and put her into the back seat ordering her to lay down. She did. Doug threw his things and bag of food on the passenger seat, got in and started the engine. They were moving, but Melodie didn't know in what direction.

"Where are we going?" she asked.

"Home, now shut up," was all he said.

Melodie looked at her new Disney Princess watch. It was 10 PM. With her belly full and the darkness of the night, she fell asleep.

Doug drove all night. He was exhausted and needed to sleep, but didn't dare stop anywhere for that long. He did stop for coffee a few times. He even picked up some pills to keep himself awake. Melodie stayed asleep. He had locked the doors. They drove all night through three states. Melodie woke up when they were in North Carolina and had to use the bathroom again. Doug found a gas station that was open, and was able to get more coffee, and some gas. He bought a bottled juice, from a vending machine, for Melodie. She was hungry and thirsty and thanked Doug for the drink, when he handed it to her.

"There are some donuts here if you want." He opened the back door and Melodie climbed in with her cold juice, Doug got into the driver's seat and set his cup in the cup holder. He pressed the door lock, picked up the box of donuts from the front seat, and handed it back to Melodie. "Here you go, kid."

Once again Melodie said, "Thank you." She took a donut from the box and ate it. She was looking out of the car windows as they drove looking for a sign to tell her where they were. Nothing looked familiar. She looked at her watch; it was 9:30AM.

Doug wanted to wait to make his next call to Lora until he had reached his destination. He estimated that to be in another twelve hours. He needed to sleep, but that would have to wait. He was running on caffeine and adrenaline. Doug put on the radio. *Perfect, a Lora Logan song.* He looked in the rear view mirror, at the child, for her reaction. She was looking at him in return, with those eyes.

Doug quickly, looked away.

Melodie heard the familiar voice of Lora on the radio. It was comforting. She looked at the mirror and saw the blue eyes of the driver looking at her. She refused to look away. He turned his attention back to the road and the business of driving. For some reason she didn't feel threatened by this stranger, only angry. She was beginning to feel more courageous. If only she could get to a phone, or get her hands on his cell phone, she could call Poppa or Lora. She sat, quietly, waiting for her opportunity. She had tried to send a silent message to the man at the gas station, but she wasn't sure whether he understood that she was mouthing, "HELP! " All he did was smile at the two of them. "What a lovely daughter you have." was what he said. The man she now knew from the news photo, who was called Douglas replied, "Thanks." and they left quickly.

Chapter 13
The Search for Melodie
9:30 AM

The Amber alert went out, almost immediately, for Melodie. There was a media frenzy in the hotel lobby, once they found out that Lora Logan was staying there. The hotel security had called in help from the local police to retain order. The story of the Logan abduction was all over TV. Lora hoped that would help in locating her daughter even more quickly. To the media she was still her sister. David issued a statement to the press and pleaded for the abductor to return his "daughter" unharmed. It was quite emotional for Lora to watch. She couldn't be there with her father because she didn't want to take attention away from the message. She wanted the focus to be on Melodies' return.

After the second phone call, Lora could hardly sleep. She was waiting for instructions as to where to meet Melodies captor. She wasn't afraid for herself, at that point, only for Melodie, having experienced the affects of his demented mind. From the police reports, she surmised that he had gotten worse, having gone undetected for so many years. It was too frightening to think about. She had to keep positive thoughts in her head to keep the negative ones from taking over.

Lora was questioning every decision she had ever made. Was she being selfish not giving Melodie up for adoption? Look at how that decision changed her parent's life. Lora couldn't imagine not having Melodie in her life. She loved her so much. She longed to hold her in her arms and kiss her sweet, soft hair. Was she selfish in wanting to go for the *Celebrity USA* contest? She could have sung and taught music in school. It would have been a good life. She wanted a better life for her parents and family. When she saw the offers coming in, while in the contest, she decided that she could do that for them. Lora was blaming herself for everything. She was building up a quilt trip.

Her father guessed what she was going through, having gone through it when this maniac attacked her, all those years ago. He and Janice were consumed with guilt for quite some time, afterward. Their priest had helped some, and they went to a counselor for a year. But now, today, with this latest turn of events, David felt rage and was consumed with thoughts of revenge. How could he comfort Lora with all this anger inside? When she looked at him, he saw the injured child that she was. He couldn't put a band-aid on this wound and kiss the pain away. He went to Rodney the next morning. "I can't just sit here and do nothing."

Just then, Rodney's phone rang. It was Justin. "He was staying at the Days Inn in Kissimmee. It looks like he left sometime last night."

Rod said, "Hang on a sec, Justin." He relayed the message to David.

"I'm going there! There might be something the police overlooked, " David told Rodney.

Rodney held up a finger indicating "wait" to David. "Are you there, now?"

Justin answered, "Yes."

"Wait there, David and I'll be right there." Rodney told the women to stay in the room. One security guard was just outside the door, one was at the elevators, while others were in the stair wells. They would be safe until he got back.

Rodney and David drove the few miles to the Days Inn. They drove around back to the room number Justin had given them. Rodney had barely stopped the car when David opened the car door and slid out. He took off running up the stairs to the room with the open door. "The police have left," Justin said, as David entered the room.

"Did they find anything?" David asked. Rod had just reached the room.

"They did the usual dusting for finger prints, and bagged up some things. It looked like ingredients to make gun powder: sugar, sulfur and potassium nitrate," Justin told them. Justin looked at Rod standing just off to the left of David. Rod nodded his head, and Justin answered. "Also, some food wrappers, a soda can, and oh, yeah, a gold bracelet."

David looked at Rodney. "Did Melodie have a bracelet?"

"Lora bought her one, as a souvenir, just yesterday. It had little charms on it," Rod answered.

"Yeah, that sounds like it could be the one," Justin commented.

"Any clues as to where they went?" David asked.

"I don't think so. I'm going to check out those wrappers I saw the police bag up. Looked like convenience type take out. There has to be some shop in this vicinity," Justin said. "I'll check back with you."

"Thanks, Justin. We're headed back to the hotel."

"Actually, Rod, I think I'd like to stick with Justin. I'm of no use to Lora back there. I need to be doing something, or at least feel like I am doing something," David told Rod. "That is if Justin will indulge me?"

Again, Justin looked to Rodney. He didn't see disapproval on Rods face. "Yeah, sure. Let's get going." He and David went to Justin's car where Justin punched in their address and then asked the GPS for any convenience stores in the area. One was a block away, so the two headed there armed with the photos of Melodie and Doug.

Emma had gotten Lora to lie down. When she looked in on her, she was asleep. She really needed to sleep. Emma had heard Rod come in early in the morning. She hoped that he was sleeping, too. The drapes in the room were still drawn from last night, not allowing the bright Florida sun in, to disturb Lora. Emma had gotten a couple hours of sleep. When she awoke she was hungry. They hadn't had any dinner. Rod tapped lightly on her door. She opened it for him. "Lora is still sleeping." Rod backed up, and Emma went into his room, pulling the door closed behind her.

"No problem. I'm glad she's getting some sleep."

"Did you learn anything?"

"Not really, Looks like either Melodie left her bracelet behind, accidentally, or on purpose. But they were gone. David is checking things out, with Justin.

"Hey, I'm hungry, Rod. Want to send down for some food?" Emma asked.

"Yeah, I could eat. What do you want?" Rod picked up the phone.

Lora walked into the room. "She wouldn't leave it behind,

accidentally. She was giving me a message. She's doing OK. Where is my father?"

"He wanted to go with Justin. He can't sit around and wait. Makes him feel useful."

"I know how he feels," Lora said.

"We were about to order something to eat," Emma told Lora.

"Just some fruit and coffee, for me." Lora went back to her room to shower. When she came back to Rod's room the food had arrived.

Rod went to the physically and emotionally drained Lora and guided her to the table by the darkened window. Emma brought a plate and set it in front of her, along with a napkin and silverware setting. Lora sighed, but did take a strawberry to eat. "Rod, eat. I can't eat all of this." Emma poured a cup of coffee and set it in front of Lora. "Thanks Emma. You're so sweet. Please sit down and eat." Rod dragged over another chair for Emma and helped her with her drink and plate. His cell phone rang.

"Hello?" Justin was calling to let him know that he and David talked to a store owner that recognized the photo of Doug. He had been in last night, very late, and had gotten two hot dogs, soda, beer, and snacks. He was on foot and alone. He never saw a little girl. Yes, they shared that information with the police. The police are scouring the neighborhood for clues, now. "Thanks Justin, keep me informed." Rod updated Lora and Emma, while they picked at their fruit.

"How will we know where they are headed?" Emma asked, which was what Lora was thinking.

"He'll use a credit card sooner or later," Rod answered, "or he'll use an ATM. We'll get him. Don't forget about the Amber alert! "Someone will spot them."

Rod had been right, Doug did have to use his credit card at a gas station in Pennsylvania, at 4:00PM. Justin had learned this from the detective on the case. "That's it! We are going back to New York. I think he's headed there." Rod had the small jet at the airport; he had flown the girls in on, readied for the flight to New York. He called Justin and told him to bring David and to meet them at the airport in two hours. The vacationers packed their belongings and got ready for the pursuit of Doug and Melodie. They would be back in New York by 9PM. Rod was hoping they would beat Rod there. The police were aware of Rod's suspicions and were on the lookout for Doug, along the route. Of course, Doug would be aware that he was being sought and not take the most direct or highly visible route.

Rod got the girls into a waiting car, in the rear of the hotel, without the media seeing them. They arrived at the airport, where Justin and David were already waiting. For security reasons, they all boarded the plane and waited there for clearance to take off. Lora's cell phone rang, making her jump with a start. "Mimi, come and take me home!" Melodie spoke softly but didn't sound frightened. That was a relief to Lora.

"I know, Baby. Poppa and I are coming for you," Lora tried to reassure her daughter.

"You don't have to look for her. I told you to meet me. We both will be waiting for you." Doug said.

"Where do you want to meet?"

"Not yet. You'll have the police waiting for me. I'll tell you when the time is right." Doug hung up.

"She sounds unharmed." Lora started to cry. "She's being very brave. I hear the strain in her voice."

David put an arm around Lora. "She has her mother's strength."

He kissed her forehead.

Rod got clearance to take off after an hour of waiting on the tarmac. Emma and Lora dozed for a bit on the flight to New York. They landed at 8:45PM at La Guardia airport. David had phoned ahead, booked four rooms at the Marriott, and arranged for a car to be waiting once they deplaned. Emma wasn't going to leave Lora's side. David also called detective Olivia Marks and arranged to have her meet them at the hotel. Lastly, he called his wife. He had been in constant touch with her, keeping her updated with each new discovery. She had wanted to join them in Florida, but David thought it would be better to stay put, not knowing where Doug was headed with Melodie. He called to let her know that they had arrived safely in New York and were ready to move at a moment's notice from the abductor. The plane was being refueled and readied. They just didn't know what this guy was thinking. They had to be ready for anything.

Justin drove the group to the hotel in a rented minivan. He dropped everyone off at the back entrance of the hotel and went to pick up some food. When he got back Rod was sleeping, and David was with the girls. Lora was in the shower in her father's room, and Emma was soaking in a tub, with her cast wrapped in plastic. David and Justin were eating some fried chicken when Detective Marks arrived at David's door. She told them about the bellhop uniform, and that was found in a dumpster near the motel where Doug was staying. We assume that's how he gained access to the hotel and why Melodie would have gone with him, willingly, to escape the fire. Laura entered the room with her long, dark hair still wet from the shower. She was wearing a white, terrycloth hotel robe and slippers. A few minutes later Emma joined the group to say her good-nights.

"Don't you want something to eat, first?" David asked, like a concerned father.

"No. Thanks. I am really tired. Be sure to wake me if anything changes, though." Said Emma.

Lora went to Emma and gave her a hug. "Thanks for staying with me. I couldn't do this alone."

"I wouldn't be anywhere else, sweetie. Promise you'll wake me if anything comes up?"

"Of course. Sleep well." Lora kissed Emma on the cheek.

"Goodnight, all." Emma turned and went into her and Lora's room, closing the door behind her.

Lora sat next to her father, on the love seat across from Justin, at the table, and Detective Marks, seated in a desk chair. "Has he been spotted anywhere, yet?" Lora asked, hopeful.

"He did use his credit card again, at a diner just over the New York border. Must have gotten dinner for the little girl."

"She has a name. Her name is Melodie," Lora corrected. She was tired and irritated with everyone. If the police had done a better job, *he* would be in jail, and this never would have happened.

"Yes, of course." Detective Marks corrected herself. "A detective is questioning the employees at the diner, as we speak." Olivia's phone rang. "Marks here," she answered. She listened carefully. "Yes, thank you detective." There was a report of a sighting, on the thruway, of the suspect's vehicle, heading west."

Lora grew pale. She knew where Doug was headed. She kept it to herself, for now. She would tell Rod, soon. She had to get him alone.

"What's wrong?" the detective asked, seeing the look on Lora's face.

"Ah, nothing. Just a little light headed I guess." She looked at

Rod. He knew something was up. I think I'll turn in for awhile. Rod knew she was trying to separate herself from everyone. He had to find out what she was up to. As soon as everyone turned in he would go to her.

"That's a good idea. We should all try and get a little sleep," Rod suggested.

Justin yawned, "I could use a few winks."

"Yeah, I guess we had better get some rest if we are going to be of any use," David said.

Detective Marks said she would call with any new developments. She left, and everyone went to their rooms. Rod was relieved to be alone. He wanted to go to Lora. He could feel that she needed him.

Chapter 14
Peace of Mind
10:00PM

Melodie was sleeping in the back seat. They had stopped for a late dinner and then an ice cream cone. Melodie chose mint chocolate chip, which was also Doug's favorite. He was discovering much about this young captive. She was very intelligent. He had caught her trying to leave clues and catch the eye of anyone that looked her way. She was a strong-willed child and very brave. Her family really loved her; it showed in her high self esteem. Doug wondered how different his life would have been if he had been loved the way she has been? Did she realize how lucky she was?

With each mile that past, Doug grew more intrigued with Melodie. He never had much contact with children. He felt a bond to her and probably more so, suspecting that she was his daughter. He knew that this was the only opportunity he would have to spend time with her. She was different than anyone he had ever met in his miserable life. She was so honest and straightforward with her thoughts. He missed her company when she was sleeping. He turned around for a moment to look at the innocent face of the sleeping girl on the back seat. She had one of his jackets pulled up to her chin. He had to turn the heat on in the car the further north they got.

Doug had considered leaving her off somewhere and taking off, at first. In the end he couldn't do it. He didn't want anything to happen to her, for one, and he needed to see her mother. She was his one chance to lure Lora Logan to him. He needed to call her. He pulled off the road, at a rest stop, and dialed her number.

Lora was sitting in her room, wondering how to get where she needed to go, when her phone rang. Lora answered on the first ring. "Hello?" She wasn't sure if it was Melodie or *him.*

"Lora?" It was him.

"Yes. Where is my baby?" She spoke softly so as not to disturb Emma.

"You mean *our* baby don't you?"

"You know?"

"Lora, I saw her eyes, and knew. You think I'm stupid?"

"Please, don't hurt her," Lora begged.

"I'm not going to hurt her, I never could," Lora was confused by this person she was talking to. He sounded different. "Are you bringing her back to me?"

"Yes, home," He answered. "I'll call in a few hours. I need to sleep."

"Can I talk to Melodie?" Lora asked.

"She's sleeping. She's so … innocent."

"I was innocent once."

"I know." He hung up.

Lora was confused. *Who was that? What kind of game was he playing, now.* She wouldn't fall for his charm, ever again. All she had to do was look over at Emma lying in bed, her face, still with fading bruises and the cast on her arm, to know to whom she was, really, just speaking with. The assault on her was as vivid, this night, as when it happened. No, he was trying to get her guard down and that wouldn't happen. She would do whatever she could to get her daughter away from that maniac. She prayed that the fact that he knew Melodie was his daughter, would keep him from hurting her. But how does the mind of a sexual predator work? She had learned that she had been his youngest victim. Maybe that was because he was not that old himself. Whatever the reason, she hoped that Melodie was just too young. She prayed for that, and for her safety.

Rod slowly opened the door to Lora and Emma's room. He didn't know if Lora would be asleep and was relieved to see her sitting in a chair in the dark. She was just staring out of the dark window. Rod saw the light from his room on her glistening cheeks. She was crying. His heart broke, and he had to go to her. He took her hands, pulled her to her feet, and held her close. He kissed her head. "This will end, and end well."

"You don't know that Rod," she sobbed, softly.

"I know I'll do whatever it takes to make that happen. Tell me what spooked you, earlier."

"I think I know where he's headed."

Rod held her back and looked into her eyes, "Where?"

"I think he's going back to the pond, where this all began; 'back to the beginning'." She said.

"Then I'm going to be there!"

"Rod, I don't want the police there. Will you take me?"

"Why don't you let me take care of this?"

"I have to go. I need to be there for Melodie. Please take me."

Rod agreed, and they slipped out of the room, without waking anyone. They decided to drive the three and a half hours to the Albany area. They would be there waiting for him. Lora fell asleep in the car, while Rod drove. She awoke when he stopped in Poughkeepsie, for gas and coffee. It was snowing lightly.

"Do you think Melodie is warm enough? She was dressed for Florida," said the concerned mother in her.

"I think she is a smart and resourceful young lady. If she was cold, she wouldn't hesitate to let someone know."

"You're right. She does have a way of getting what she wants." She was thinking, *not unlike her father, then* she rebuked herself for the thought. She grew quiet again.

"Baby, she'll be fine." Rod reached over and squeezed Lora's hand. Lora laid her head on Rod's shoulder.

"Rod, when I get my baby back, will this be the end, forever?"

"I'll see to that. You can count on it. Trust me to do whatever is necessary."

"I can't live with the possibility of him getting at anyone I love, again."

"You won't have to. I'll put an end to this, once and for all. For you and those you love."

Lora brought Rod's hand to her mouth and kissed his fingers. "I feel so safe with you. For the first time since this happened, I truly feel safe and hopeful."

Rod pulled her hand to his mouth and kissed it with his full, warm lips. "There's nothing I wouldn't do for you, or your daughter. You know that, right?" He hesitated before saying what he had been holding back for so long. "Lora, I love you." Then he immediately regretted it. Was it a mistake? Was Lora ready to hear those words?

Lora didn't respond right away. She couldn't believe what she just heard. How long she dreamed to hear a man tell her that. She laid her head on his shoulder again and softly said, "I love you, too."

Rod slowed the car and pulled over to the side of the road that was deserted, at the hour. He took Lora in his arms and kissed her. The snow was falling heavier now and the wipers, on low, couldn't keep up with it. The passengers inside didn't notice. "Are you sure about this?" Rod asked, after their passionate kiss.

"I didn't think I'd ever want a man to hold me or kiss me. Then, thank God, you came into my life. You've stirred feelings inside me I never knew I had. " Rod kissed her again. "I can't believe this is happening." She smiled up at Rod. "You make me so happy."

"Well, as wonderful as this is, we should get going." Rod turned the wipers on high and cleared the windshield, before signaling and pulling back onto the highway.

Lora's cell phone rang. "Hello? Dad, I'm fine. I'm with Rod." Her father asked about three or four questions, in quick succession. "Dad, slow down. Everything is going to be fine. Let me call you back later." She hung up on her father. "I suspect he knows where we're headed."

That's when Rod's phone rang. "Want to bet on who that is?" He smiled at Lora. He answered the phone, "Mr. Logan, sir." Lora could hear her father's loud voice, but not his words. "I'd rather you not alert the police, just yet. Their presence might scare him off. Lora will be safe." Some more words from her father. "Mr. Logan, Let me call you back. I am trying to drive, and it's snowing hard. I wouldn't want to have an accident." A pause, then, "Yes sir, as soon as possible."

"He's just concerned for our safety." Lora said in defense of her father. "Mine and Melodie's that is."

"The thing is I can understand where he's coming from. I'm just not ready to alert the police."

"And I thank you for that. They haven't been very successful, as far as I can see. Look how long this guy has been out there, assaulting women and doing who knows what else."

Rod saw the exit for Albany. "You'll have to help me out now. Where to?"

Lora gave directions as Rod drove. She hadn't been back to this area in nine years. The nearer she got to the farm the more distraught she became. Rod felt her tension. Twenty minutes later, Lora directed him to the dirt road that led to the pond. It was not plowed and was covered with fresh snow. There were no tire marks. Rod hoped that they had beaten Doug there. They would lay in wait. Doug drove in as far as he dared and pulled off to the side as far as he was able safely, before killing the engine and lights.

"It's going to get cold in here. No telling how long we'll have to wait." Rod removed his seatbelt, reached over the seat, and pulled a blanket from the back seat to cover Lora. "This will help." The windows were quickly becoming opaque from the snow. It was dark inside the car, but it wouldn't be long before daybreak. It was already 4:30AM. "Are you warm enough?" He asked.

"I'm fine. I hope I'm right about this. I hope this is where he is headed. Oh God! I just want my baby girl back."

Rod put his large hand on the side of Lora's desperate face, and she leaned into it. "I am going to see that that's what happens baby."

"Please let her be OK. You don't think he would harm her, do you?" Lora's eyes were pleading.

Rod wanted to hold her and promise everything would be fine, but how could he. Anything could happen when you are dealing with a psychopath. "I think Melodie is one tough little girl." was all he could say, in all honesty.

Doug was heading to the farm. Melodie was still sleeping on the seat. The sky was beginning to brighten to a light gray in the winter, morning light. It was still snowing lightly. Everything was covered in a fresh, white blanket of snow. He dialed Lora's number for the last time.

Lora answered on the first ring. "The beginning of the end. Come get the girl."

"Where is she?" Lora asked.

"Now is not the time for games." Doug's voice sounded tired and angry. "You knew I'd go back to the beginning."

"Yes. I'm already there."

Doug smiled. The only bitch he ever met with a brain. "I hope you're alone."

"I didn't tell the police if that's what you're asking. I didn't even tell my father."

"But you're not alone?"

"No."

"I didn't think you would be. He better keep his distance."

"He won't interfere. Just give me my daughter and leave. That's all I want."

"No thoughts of revenge?"

"I'm not going to lie, I hate you. God, how I hate you." Lora was shaking from anger and the cold.

Doug had stopped at the beginning of the road to the pond and looked around for signs of anyone.

"I can think of a reason why you shouldn't hate me. I'm looking at her."

"Make no mistake, Melodie is mine. All mine." Lora was so angry.

"Her eyes say something different to me."

Lora couldn't control her anger any longer."Give me my daughter, you bastard!" Rodney reached for the phone, but Lora pulled away.

Doug smiled and started down the road to the pond. The snow was deeper making driving difficult. The car slid a little even though he was going slowly. He pulled to the side; shut off the engine, the headlights, and reached for the glove box. He popped it opened and pulled out a knife he had concealed there earlier. His plan was working nicely. Lora was here. All he had to do was get rid of the goon. They would be alone again.

Melodie woke up. "Where are we?" she asked, rubbing her eyes with the palms of her hands.

Doug clicked the glove box shut. "Back at the beginning."

Melodie strained to see out of the car window. "It's snowing in Disney?" She asked bewildered.

"What? No!" She had misunderstood. "You'll understand someday kid. Now let's go find Lora."

"Oh! Lora is here? Can I wear your jacket? I'm cold." She hurriedly stuffed her arms into the oversized denim jacket without waiting for an answer. Doug just shook his head. "I don't have any boots. Is poppa here, too?" she asked, wrapping the jacket around her small body. The arms hung longer than her arms, hiding her hands.

"The only one that matters." he answered. "Don't worry, I'll carry you." He got out and pushed his door shut. He went around to her door and opened it with his left hand, while slipping the knife into his back pants pocket with his right hand.

Lora and Rod heard the car door closing They couldn't see, but they knew who it was. "Stay here!" She told Rod.

"I don't think so." Rod started to open his door."

"Let me do this." Lora said firmly. "He knows you're here with me. What's he going to do?" Lora opened her door. Rod grabbed her left arm and looked at her with grave concern.

"Please Lora, I don't trust him. I don't want anything to happen to you."

She put her hand over his, "I don't either, but I'm going to get my daughter. I think I'm the only one who can. Let my father know."

Rod, reluctantly, let go of her arm, but didn't take his watchful eyes from her. He called David and told him what was happening and where they were. Lora got out of the car and closed the door. She stood there, in the early morning light, straining to see through the now, heavy snow. Rod had turned the car's ignition to axillary power in order to operate the wipers. He couldn't see anyone outside through the snow fall. Rod knew it would be worse if he turned on the lights. Lora took a few guarded steps away from the car. She was secretly glad it was winter. It hid the familiar look of her last summer here. It felt as if she was somewhere else. She called out for her daughter before continuing. "Melodie?"

"Mimi!" came the excited, welcomed response. Warm tears fell from Lora's eyes onto her cold cheeks.

"Mel! I'm here, baby!" She hurried now, through the foot deep snow, toward the sound of her daughter's voice.

Rod was watching from inside the car.

A silhouette came towards Lora. She was confused by the image at first, then realized it was Doug carrying Melodie through the snow. He stopped ten feet from her. Melodie was hanging around his neck with both arms, as if she belonged there. As if she was comfortable with this monster. Lora felt nauseous. "Put her down!" she yelled at Doug.

"Come here and get her. She doesn't have boots." *As if Doug would care about such a thing,* Lora thought.

Rod was listening from inside the car. He had rolled down his window for that purpose. He could read people and body language. He knew Doug was going to try something. Rod had his loaded gun out with the safety off. Whatever this guy was thinking, he wouldn't allow him to act on it. Lora started towards her daughter, taking long strides through the deep snow, and moving as fast as she could.

"Mimi!" her excited daughter called. Melodie let go of Doug's neck with one arm in order to reach out to Lora. "Mimi, I missed you. Where's Poppa and Momma?"

Lora was close now. When she reached out for her daughter, Doug quickly set her down and grabbed Lora's arm. "Not so fast. We need to talk."

Melodie looked at Doug and then Lora. She was confused.

"Mel, go to my car. Mr. Rod is waiting for you." When Melodie didn't move Lora said more sternly, "NOW! I'll be right there." Lora noticed a glint from the knife in Doug's hand, now.

Melodie turned, to struggle through the snow, towards the car. She saw Rod standing next to it.

Rod saw her coming and called out to her. "Come on Mel."

She saw him hold out his hand and hurried to the car. "Hi, Mr. Rod." Rod had started the engine and turned on the heat. "Get in and stay here where it's warm, honey. I'm going to get Lora. Keep the door closed and locked, OK sweetheart?" He didn't want to alarm her. He knew she had been through a lot already.

"OK, Mr. Rod." She climbed in the back. Rod closed the door, then headed towards Lora. "Let her go now right now, Douglas!" He hadn't seen the knife, yet.

"Stay right there! Lora and I got to have a little talk. Don't we now?" Doug pulled Lora in front of him and held the knife to her throat.

Rod stopped short. The gun was in the pocket of his jacket. He had his hand on it. Doug pulled Lora back in the direction of the pond. Doug couldn't tell where he was going, He was just backing away from him.

"Look! I stopped. Stay where you are." Rod yelled back. Rod didn't know that the pond was in that direction, never having been here. Lora was backwards, but knew the pond was in the direction they were going. It should be frozen. She hoped so, anyway.

Doug backed up another couple of feet before stopping. "There was always something special about you." Doug spoke softly to Lora.

"Please, let me go, my daughter needs me." Lora pleaded.

"Yes, children need their mother's. Sometimes children get the wrong mother's, and they never had a choice."

"I'm sorry if you didn't have a good childhood, Melodie deserves better."

"Say it!, Call it like it is. *My daughter* deserves better."

"I can't think of her that way. She is and always has been *MY* daughter."

"Why didn't you get an abortion?"

Rod couldn't hear what they were saying in their hushed voices. He was going on body language. So far Doug wasn't acting any more threatening. He stepped forward in order to try and hear better. Doug saw the advance. "Hey!. Stay put, asshole!" Doug stepped back again. Lora put up her hand to signal 'wait' to Doug.

"All right!, Just let Lora go."

"Answer me! I want to know why you had her."

"Life is precious," was all she said.

"Life sucks. And you're a fool if you believe otherwise."

"Melodie has a wonderful life, with people who love and protect her."

"She is living a lie. You're living a lie."

"She's too young for the truth."

" What do you tell her about her father? She must ask."

"I just said he's gone. She's too young for any more than that."

"What will you tell her, when she's older?"

Lora had to think. She wasn't sure what she would say. That
time was too far into the future. She knew she didn't want to upset
this mad man any further. "I guess I'd tell her that he was a sad and
desperate soul."

Doug laughed at that. Rod got nervous. "That's enough! Let
Lora go!"

Doug looked at Rod and saw the gun pointed at him, now. He
smiled. "You won't shoot and take a chance of hitting her. I've seen
the way you look at her." Still holding the knife to her throat, he
placed Lora a little more in front of himself. Lora had her hands
on his arm. Feeling Doug slip, she spun out of his grip. Doug had
slipped on the snow covered bank. He slid down a foot to the frozen pond. He was scrambling to stand up on the snow covered ice,
still holding the knife.

Rod took the opportunity to rush forward and grab Lora just
as she was falling. He pulled her to standing and ordered her to the
car. Lora didn't hesitate. She hurried to her daughter. When she
reached the car she told Melodie to unlock the door. She opened
the door and looked back to see Doug running, slipping across the

pond with Rod closing in on him. She climbed in next to Melodie, wrapped her daughter in her arms, and kissed her all over head and face. "Are you OK? He didn't hurt you, did he?"

"No, I'm OK."

Lora looked up to see Rod and Doug struggling. Rod had a size advantage, but Doug had the knife. She saw the blade glistening in the morning light. The sun was getting a little brighter now.

Rod had reached Doug. He tackled him from behind, after putting his gun back in his pocket. He was so tempted to use it on this guy. *Not in front of the child,* he thought. Doug twisted around, slashing out at Rod with his knife. He sliced through Rods jacket. Then he stabbed out and cut Rod in the right arm.

Although Rod was wounded, his adrenaline and determination kept him going. "You aren't going to get away this time, asshole." He struck out at Doug with all the force he could muster with his left arm, hitting him in the head.

Doug's head went back and hit the ice. That still didn't slow him down. He thrust the knife again this time into Rod's stomach. He lost hold of the knife and they both heard a cracking. The ice was giving way beneath their combined weight. Rod was able to pull the knife from his stomach just before the ice opened up, swallowing the two men.

Lora was watching from the car and saw the two go down, through the ice, and out of sight. She slid out of the car and rushed to the bank. "Rodney!" She screamed. "Oh my God, RODNEY!" Lora looked back at the car just as Melodie started to get out. "Get in the car! Please Mel. Stay in the car!"

Lora started to take a step down to the ice. She slipped and slid the rest of the way to the icey surface. The ice held her, though. She heard the frightened Melodie call from behind her.

CELEBRITY

"MIMI!"

"I'm all right! Stay there. Call 911 and get help. My phone is on the seat. Tell them Murray Farm Pond" In the distance she saw a head come up through the hole in the ice. It was Rodney. Thank God! "Rodney!" She called out to him.

Rodney was sputtering. He was trying to reach out for some solid ice. "For God's sake, stay there." He yelled to her.

Lora stopped. "How can I help?" she called back. It was light enough, now, for her to see the water turning red around Rod's head. "You're hurt. What should I do?" She laid down flat on her stomach and tried to slide her body closer, through the deep snow. Lora tried to stay in the guys footsteps, but still had to wave her arms back and forth to brush the snow aside. She could hear Rod falling back into the frigid water and splashing to grasp hold of something, anything, to pull himself out. Lora got close enough to feel the wet ice on her chest. She extended her arm as far as she could. "Grab my hand!" she told Rod. The water and snow was red around her. Rod reached out to her. She grabbed hold of his icy hand but it slipped away and Rod went under again. He came up again and she saw his teeth chattering. "Try again!" she said. Rod reached with his good arm and this time caught hold of Lora's wrist. She clamped down on his wrist in return with both hands. "Come on baby," she encouraged him. She pulled back. Rod came out of the water to his chest but slipped back again. Lora didn't let go. She was like a pit bull and was growing more determined. She pulled again and Rod came up. This time the ice held his weight. Lora gave another tug. Rodney slid onto the ice and lie still, breathing hard. Blood was flowing out around him.

Rod couldn't feel his legs. They were numb with cold. Lora sat up and began to pull Doug's limp body across the ice. She painstakingly inched her way back towards the bank, on her butt, until she got Rod to the bank's edge.

"Come on baby, help me here." She stood up and tried to help Rod to stand. He managed to grab hold of a tree on the bank and assist Lora in getting him up the bank. When he was safely on the ground. Lora ran to the car and got the blanket from the front seat. She took it back to Rod and tugged at his wet frozen jacket, peeling it from his shaking body. She wrapped the blanket around him. They heard the sirens coming down the road. Rod was lying unconscious, now. He had lost a lot of blood and was suffering from hypothermia.

"Please God!, Don't let him die," Lora cried, as they loaded Rod into the ambulance. They wrapped Lora in a blanket and put her in the ambulance too. Lora sat on the bench seat with her daughter beside her, wrapped in the blanket. She was watching the paramedics work on the unconscious Rod. She had told them there was another man that went under and never surfaced. The police were still at the scene, when they were driven away to the hospital. Her father had called Detective Marks, and the local police were dispatched to the farm.

When the ambulance reached the hospital, Rod was whisked away to one cubicle and Lora to another, in the emergency room. A nurse took charge of Melodie. Melodie still had her mother's cell phone and pushed speed dial to call David, who answered on the first ring, "Lora?" Her name came up on his screen.

"Poppa?" Melodie said.

"Oh my God Mel! Where are you honey? Is Lora with you?"

"Poppa, we're in the hospital."

David tried to remain calm, for Melodies' sake. " Are you all right?"

"Yes, I'm fine. Mr. Rod is hurt bad" She told David.

She sounded so young. "How is Lora?"

She isn't hurt. She's with the doctor. Poppa can you come get us?"

"Who 's with you, Honey? Give the phone to whoever is with you."

Melodie held the phone to the nurse. "Poppa wants to talk to you."

The nurse took the phone and explained to David the condition of his daughter. She wouldn't give him any information on Rodney, because he wasn't family. He told the nurse he would contact Rod's sister, which he did as soon as he hung up. He told her he would pick her up and drive her to the hospital in Albany. Rebeca phoned the hospital and learned that Rod had multiple knife wounds and was being taken to surgery. Three hours later David, Emma and Rod's sister walked through the Albany Medical Center hospital. Justin had sped the whole way. He dropped them off and went to see what the police knew.

Lora was dressed in a hospital gown, robe, and paper slippers with a blanket on her lap. She was in the waiting room with her arms around Melodie. She never wanted to let go of her daughter again. She saw her father and Emma walking towards them and stood up to accept the embrace from her father. Emma hugged Melodie, then they switched. "Thank God you're unharmed. Your mother and I have been out of our minds with worry. Did the police get there in time, honey?"

"Dad, not now. Please. I'm so worried about Rodney." She put her arm around Melodie and sat back down.

"I know, I'm sorry. Have you heard anything?"

"He's still in surgery."

Emma sat next to Lora and Melodie. "Can I get either of you anything? I'm going to get a coffee."

"Oh Emma that sounds great! Thank you. Melodie, how about a hot cocoa?" Lora asked the girl snuggled next to her. Melodie nodded her head. David sat down next to Lora and put his arm around both of the girls, relieved that they were alive.

Rebeca, Rod's sister, came over and sat across from them. She had stopped at the desk to see what she could learn about Rod. "They don't know how much longer. A doctor will come out as soon as they can." She sounded distraught.

Lora reached forward and touched Rebeca's knee. "He's a fighter. He's got to pull through." Rebeca just nodded her head slightly in agreement. Emma returned with a tray of paper cups, with white plastic lids. Rebeca hopped up and offered to help her with them , because she was struggling, with only one good hand. Rebeca took the tray from Emma and set it on a table next to her. Emma had gotten a coffee for everyone and Melodie's hot cocoa. The adults set about preparing their coffee's with the creamers and sugars provided. David wanted to know what had occurred but didn't want to discuss it in front of Melodie.

Emma was very intuitive and suspected that David wanted to talk to Lora. "Hey Mel, I'm hungry for some lunch. Want to go to the cafeteria with me?"

Melodie looked to David and Lora. David answered, "I think that's a great idea. Bring back some sandwiches for us while you're at it Kiddo."

"Okay, Poppa." Emma held out her hand to Melodie, and the two walked down the hall, side by side.

As soon as David knew the two were out of hearing, he took Lora by the shoulders and turned her slightly to face him. "Lora, tell me what happened. How did you know where he would be? I suspected that myself. I even told Detective Marks."

Lora looked at her father. "He called and it was something he said about the beginning. I knew he meant the pond, so Rod and I went there to meet him."

"Then what happened." Rebeca was listening and looking from one to the other.

"Well, I was right. We beat him there. He showed up with Mel and when I went to get her from him, he grabbed me. He had a knife at my throat."

"My God Lora! Why did Rod allow you to go by yourself?"

"Rod was angry. He didn't trust him. He tried to stop me. I had to do it. I had to get my daughter from that mad man."

Rebeca put her hand to her mouth to stifle a small gasp.

"Then what happened. Honey?" David was holding Lora's hands in his.

"When Doug grabbed me, Rod got Mel into the car and came towards us. Doug pulled me back. When he lost his balance on the bank of the pond, I started to fall. Rod rushed in and pulled me out of harm's way. I ran to the car with Mel. Rod took off across the ice after that mad man. I don't even think Rod knew he was on ice. They struggled and the next thing I knew the both of them went down through the ice. The rest is pretty much a blur."

"How did Rod get out of the water?"

"I guess I pulled him out. I do remember telling Mel to call for help."

"What about that mad man?"

"I never saw him come back up." David pulled Lora close and she buried her head in his chest and wept. "Daddy, he has to pull through. He just has to." David knew she was speaking of Rodney.

"You two have gotten very close, haven't you."

"I don't know what I'd do without him. I never thought I could trust a man. But Rod is the kindest, most gentle, soul I have ever known. I feel so safe and secure with him."

A somber faced doctor approached them. Rebeca stood and the doctor asked if she was Rodney Blackman's sister. When she answered "Yes." The doctor told her that Rodney had made it through the surgery. He had lost a great deal of blood and they were able to repair the damage to his stomach. The next 24 hours would be crucial. Rebeca thanked the doctor and asked if she could see Rod. The doctor said yes, Rod was in recovery and she could go in for a few minutes. Rebeca turned and looked at Lora. I'll just be a minute and then you can have some time with him. Lora nodded slightly. Rebeca turned and went to the recovery room. She only stayed a couple of minutes, as promised, and then returned.

"Lora, go sit with him." She touched Lora on the arm.

"Thank you, Rebeca." She breathed softly, and rushed down the hallway to the recovery room. She pushed the door open, silently. Rod lay still, under a white blanket and sheets. His right forearm was bandaged and he had an IV in the left arm. A nurse was taking his blood pressure and charting it. "How's he doing?" Lora asked her.

"He hasn't woken up yet," She answered,

Lora went to the bed and picked up his right hand, as she sat in a nearby chair. She brought the hand to her lips. "Please get better. I need you." Lora put his hand on her tear covered cheek Lora held Rod's hand and said a prayer for his recovery. After some time, she saw Rod's eyes move slightly. "That's it, Baby. Wake up." His eyes moved and began to flutter open. When they finally opened, Lora said "Hi babe," and smiled.

"Hi" Rod said. "Please don't cry."

"I'm just so happy you're alive," she said wiping her cheeks with her left hand. She was still holding his hand in her right.

"Me too. I think I have you to thank for that. The client saves the body guard. Not exactly what I want to put on my resume." He smiled. "What happened to Douglas?" Rod started to cough.

"Stop talking and rest."

"Did he get rescued too?"

"No." then she corrected herself. "I don't know. The police are still there as far as I know. Just rest now and get better. I don't know how I could go on if anything happened to you."

Lora wiped more tears from her face.

Rod was weak but pulled her hand to his lips and kissed it. "Nothing is going to happen to me. I have so much to live for." Then he added, "Now." He paused to rest for a moment. "Hey, thanks for saving me." He had to rest again before speaking. "When I get out of here, would you go away with me? Just the two of us. Away from everyone and everything. Let's see if we have anything to build on, here."

The nurse came in and told Lora her time was up. She stood, reluctantly, leaned over Rod and spoke softly, "I'll go to the ends of the earth with you." She kissed his lips. "I'll be back. You need your rest."

Rod was in the hospital for a week. Lora sat with him every day. The police took their statements and told her they never recovered a second body. They would resume their search when the ice melted. Doug was officially presumed dead. Her nightmare was over, and she and Emma could have peace of mind once again. At least that was how they saw it.

The media got ahold of the whole tragic story and hounded Lora for interviews. David hired Justin to help keep the press away from Lora, while Rodney was recuperating. Her publicist, Paul released a statement to the press. He told the world of Lora's tragic story. Lora went on tour and was even more popular, after her story came out.

Lora, David, and Janice sat down with Melodie and told her as much of the story as she was old enough to handle. They didn't mention that Doug had fathered her. That information could wait until she was older. They just told her that the man that took her was very sick and had died that night. He wouldn't come back for her again. That seemed to set her mind at ease. She returned to her precocious, yet charming ways and went on tour with Lora, when she wasn't in school, this time as her daughter. Melodie became very popular at school. All of her friends loved Lora's music. Melodie brought autographed CD's for her friends.

Rod spent a couple of months recuperating at his sister's. He was dying to be with Lora, but knew she needed some time for healing, herself. They talked every day. Rod also stayed in touch with the Albany detectives. There was still no sign of Doug's body. They had no plans of draining the pond. Douglas Civics was declared dead; case closed.

Rod joined Lora and Melodie, when they went to Europe, for the first part of the tour. Lora appeared in ten cities in two weeks. It was both hectic and thrilling. Melodie loved every minute of it. She loved spending time with her mother and Rod. Rod was becoming a father figure to her, and he basked in the roll. Melodie was allowed to drop the Mr. and address him as Rod. They took in the tourist sites in London, (and) visited the castles and wineries, along the Rhine River in Germany. They climbed to the top of the Eiffel

Tower and toured the Louvre Museum in Paris. Rod and Lora had a romantic dinner along the Seine.

At the end of their two week, whirl-wind trip, they took Melodie back to the Logan ranch. She stayed with David and Janice, while Rod and Lora took a week for themselves, before her USA tour began. She wouldn't have another break for six months, at which time she would go home for the holidays. Rod booked a villa at Far Toryuga in the Caymen Islands. It came with a private beach, fresh water pool, and gazebo. It was the perfect place to hide away from the world; paradise. They took long walks on the beach, and went skinny dipping in the private pool in the evening. They had drinks in the gazebo, on a lazy afternoon. They were enjoying each other, learning about each other, and loving each other. Life was easy here. Loving was very easy.

The Tiki bar on the beach was crowded. Bikini clad women lay in lounge chairs, walked along the water's edge, and crowded the small bar. Some were in the company of men, some were alone. The couple sitting on stools at the bar had been there for about an hour. They enjoyed each other's conversation. They laughed and drank their drinks. She wore a turquoise bikini and a large sun hat. She smelled of suntan oil. Her skin was a deep bronze color from hours in the Mediterranean sun and glistened with the oil. His skin was getting darker by the hour. His hair was getting blonder. The girl giggled at something he said. He tucked a stray strand of hair behind her ear. She leaned towards his hand with her head. It was a small but intimate gesture between two friendly strangers. She traced the scar on his arm, with her finger, wondering how he got it but not asking. It was too soon to get so personal. She was here to have a good time. He was here for something else.

He looked at her through his blue eyes hidden behind dark

glasses. They all looked like Lora now. They all had long dark hair and innocent faces. He kept tabs on Lora's life and career. He knew her every move; except where she was right now. Their paths would cross again. He knew it. She was unaware, and that suited him just fine. Until then, he would make do with little bimbos like this one, giggling at nothing,and flaunting herself. He knew what she wanted, and he is just the one to give it to her. He helped her slip off the stool and offered her his arm, to escort her from the bar. She was a bit wobbly. She had too much to drink. It didn't matter. He took off her hat as they walked, and her shiny, long dark hair fell around her shoulders. Yeah, nothing matters, she'll do. Stupid girl won't even remember. He smiled as he escorted her to his car. And tomorrow he would be somewhere else. This was paradise.

Also by Kathleen Squire Merolla

The Revelation
Miracle Mountain

Breinigsville, PA USA
08 December 2010
250866BV00003B/18/P

9 781432 756277